MR CRUMBLESTONE'S EDEN

Pressures and inhumanities may drive a man of peace to become an unwilling criminal . . . Henry Crumblestone was a quiet little man who would never knowingly have harmed another, and it was a dreadful twist of irony that caused him to kill in defence of a dream. Mr. Crumblestone thought he had found his own secret Eden, but — as it was in the beginning — there were serpents in Eden, and even a man like Mr Crumblestone could not endure serpents for ever.

*Books by Alan Stewart Well
in the Linford Mystery Library:*

CANDICE IS DEAD

ALAN STEWART WELL

Mr Crumblestone's Eden

Complete and Unabridged

LINFORD
Leicester

First published in Great Britain in 1980

First Linford Edition
published 1997

British Library CIP Data

Well, Alan Stewart
 Mr Crumblestone's Eden.—Large print ed.—
 Linford mystery library
 1. English fiction—20th century
 2. Large type books
 I. Title
 823.9'14 [F]

 ISBN 0–7089–5027–2

Published by
F. A. Thorpe (Publishing) Ltd.
Anstey, Leicestershire

Set by Words & Graphics Ltd.
Anstey, Leicestershire
Printed and bound in Great Britain by
T. J. Press (Padstow) Ltd., Padstow, Cornwall

This book is printed on acid-free paper

1

THERE was an atmosphere of subdued excitement in Courtroom number two of the Wiscliffe Crown Court. The Judge, His Honour Judge Thomas Deeping-Sproate, bewigged, scarlet robed and with prominent flushed patches on his solemn face, gazed outwards over the cluttered rectangle of his domain.

The Judge's lay companion, Mrs Mabel Deane, J.P., sat and wriggled in the tall-backed, leather upholstered chair at his side, a handsome chair, built more for ostentation than for comfort. Mrs Deane was simpering as she basked in the glory of her day. It was an honour — not to mention a privilege — to share with this severe but widely respected adjudicator the responsibility of sitting in judgment on her fellow creatures and Mrs Deane

1

was acutely conscious of it.

Today, she held true power. She was reluctant to admit, even to herself, that whatever the outcome of the day's cases and no matter how much he might invite her views in the privacy of his retiring-room, the final decisions would always rest with Deeping-Sproate.

Mr Haslington, the learned Clerk, huddled in his seat a modest tier below the Judge and, with his chin buried in his snowy bat-wing collar, toyed idly with a ball-point pen, which he advanced and retracted endlessly in a series of audible clicks. Haslington had just instructed the prisoner to stand in order to receive sentence and there would be nothing more for him to do until after His Honour had made his pronouncement.

The ladies and gentlemen of the jury — empanelled to hear an entirely different case which had yet to start — had listened to the evidence as outlined briefly by the perspiring Counsel and they waited with much curiosity to hear the Judge hand out a right old pasting to the audacious criminal in the Dock. The Counsel — their duty done — relaxed in sprawling attitudes on the foremost row of cross-benches, scarcely interested enough to look up.

Henry Crumblestone had pleaded guilty.

Guilty, had been the only possible plea in the circumstances. The evidence against him was strong and the outcome inescapable. When committing the crimes he had acted quite recklessly, sparing no thought for the inevitable punishment as it was bound to affect himself. He had wanted the world to know the nature of his transgressions and the motives which had driven him to perpetrate them.

Cynics, speaking of it since, had suggested that capture, arraignment and consequential publicity had been amongst his primary aims, and the more Henry considered that suggestion the less inclined he was to deny its truth.

Now, as he waited in a detached way

to hear what was to become of him, he felt no fear, no unbearable strain, only a warm feeling of satisfaction in a job well done. True, there had been a certain unfortunate and unintended side effect, and if he allowed his mind to dwell on that, his satisfaction diminished, but his main purpose had been achieved and the rest would have to be borne.

The Judge had begun to speak now and his words intruded on Henry's thoughts. He listened because he was involved.

"Henry Crumblestone," Deeping-Sproate boomed. "You have pleaded guilty to two very serious crimes and it is my duty to reflect your wickedness in the penalty I impose. It has been brought most eloquently to my notice by your Counsel that by admitting the charges you have eased the work of this Court. That may very well be so. Indeed, the facts as outlined do suggest that since your arrest you have not sought to evade the consequences of your misdeeds. I have noted the

4

fact, but I am bound also to note that you have shown yourself to be entirely unrepentant. Not once, either at your appearance before the Lower Court or since the start of this trial, either by word or deed, have you expressed the slightest regret . . . "

Regret?

Henry Crumblestone allowed that single word to sneak in, before closing his mind to the ramblings of the Judge. It was true he had never expressed regret, but then — apart from that dreadful side issue — he had never felt regret. The things he had done were things he had set out to do, and Henry was not the kind of dishonest person who might profess an emotion he did not feel. How many others, he wondered, amongst the rag-tag army of people caught up in the meshes of his downfall, had felt regret?

Basil Jenks, for example. Had Jenks felt any regret?

The question was a very pertinent one. In the elaborate farce which had culminated in this trial, Jenks had been Henry's main adversary, perhaps his *only* adversary if the truth ever came to light, and Henry knew beyond mistake that Jenks had felt a bucketful of ill will at the time. He had bitterly resented the injury done to him and had shouted his rage to all who would listen. If a name were needed for that most gratifying hatred Henry had managed to rouse in the breast of Basil Jenks, then *regret* would serve as well as any other. And if Henry himself had ever felt regret, it was certainly not for any unpleasantness Jenks might have suffered.

As for poor, doddery old Sam Little . . . Henry shifted his gaze to look with affection on a tall, gaunt, elderly man with brown features and a huge shock of grey hair, who sat, motionless, in the Public Gallery . . . Sam, the fascinating old-timer and companion for only a few months, had been shamefully cut-up about the whole business, or so it had been reported.

Sam himself had not said so. Indeed, there hadn't been a single word out of Sam since their last chatty hour beside the river and Henry was a little peeved about that. Though to be fair there had been no real opportunity, and Henry felt quite sure the old man had not deserted him.

Henry had twice been arraigned before the Bench at Wiscliffe Magistrates' Court, once for a brief remand hearing and once again at the committal proceedings when the formality of transferring his trial to a higher court had been completed. Sam Little had been present on each occasion, his face wrinkled with sadness, and each time they had exchanged looks full of meaning. But he had made no move to approach Henry in the Dock, nor had he communicated in any other way during the waiting weeks.

But no matter, his presence alone was a comfort, and he was there as a friend. Others might come to witness

Henry's eclipse or to feed their ghoulish curiosity, but not Sam Little. If all he wanted was to know the result, he could read about it in the newspapers. The story would be well publicised if the bowed heads and scribbling pencils in the Press seats were any guide.

Make no mistake, Sam was there because he wanted to be there, sitting like a faithful dog in the body of the Court, eyes fixed earnestly on the Judge and ears receptive to the words issuing from the lips of that dominant legal figure.

Sam had felt regret. Sam was still feeling regret.

And that very nearly exhausted the list.

It hardly mattered to count crabby little Frank Finch or Joan Westwell Crumblestone, Henry's wife. If either could have attended they would have done so out of spite, finding malicious pleasure in his fall from grace, and Henry would have hated that. But they were not present, and if one or both

8

had felt regret it would have changed nothing.

And Miss Dawkins? Mary?

She was a casting from a very different mould.

Mary had wept softly beyond the wire-mesh of the visiting hall on the one occasion she had seen him while on remand. She had begged to be allowed to visit again, but Henry — still the employer laying down rules for his staff — had forbidden it. And Mary had accepted the rebuff and still remained loyal enough to attend today's hearing other than in a spirit of pique. Even now as he watched her, sitting right at the back of the Courtroom and almost hidden from his view by a thick plaster pillar, she kept dabbing her eyes with a balled handkerchief held in her pink fist.

Yes, undoubtedly Mary Dawkins was feeling regret — or some other brand of sadness. And for Mary, Henry Crumblestone felt a kind of sadness too, but it was not regret.

Strange how his actions had affected so many lives as well as his own. And strange, too, how everything had come about so quickly. A year ago, Henry would never have believed himself capable of such anti-social conduct. At heart, he had always been law-abiding to a fault. He respected the ordered society in which he lived and worked, respected the rights of other people and whole-heartedly supported the Rule of Law. As a practising Solicitor — albeit concerned primarily with Company Law — he could hardly have been otherwise.

And yet he had transgressed the law most seriously — so much could not possibly be denied — and that must have surprised a great many people apart from himself. In particular, Mr Tomlinson, the leading partner in his firm, must have been terribly shocked when he learned that . . .

" . . . your employer has spoken very favourably of your loyalty and industry and has expressed complete surprise at your behaviour," His Honour Judge Deeping-Sproate was saying, "and Mr Simmons, the Probation Officer, has done likewise. I have taken all those matters into account, but I cannot ignore the extreme seriousness of the offences to which you have quite properly pleaded guilty and it is therefore my intention to pass upon you a sentence commensurate with the gravity of your crimes. The sentence of this Court is . . . "

His Honour tended to drone.

Henry Crumblestone fixed his eyes on the gilt-and-white plaster cherub which adorned the far right hand corner of the Courtroom ceiling and saw himself back where everything had begun.

2

HE was peacefully afloat.

The spring sun spread its warmth and glitter on the smooth brown waters of the River Wissey, picking out the shiny red splotch of the Club's punt which was anchored in slack water, almost completely surrounded by lily-pads. Seated firmly on the centre-board with feet propped against the gunwale, Henry Crumblestone glanced pridefully at the brave curve of his rod and the cobweb shimmer of his line as another fish fought its way into his hands.

One last cast and it would be time to leave.

Expertly, Henry flicked his wrist and sent his light tackle soaring outwards, to land with a plop in a clear patch among the lily-pads. The right spot exactly. There the crushed bread-and-biscuit mixture had been strewn in sparing gobs and there the hungry shoals had started to congregate. A size twenty hook, encased in single yellow maggot, followed three spaced dust shot into the depths of the hole and his float — a mere inch of thin peacock quill — cocked and settled low, leaving only its bright red tip to dimple the surface.

There was no appreciable current.

Henry glued his eyes to the float, which rode static for half a minute and then dipped sharply. He struck at once, smiling as he felt a responsive wiggle from somewhere in the depths. A nice roach by the feel of it. Coming, coming, damn! The fish had nosed a reed and slipped free of the hook.

Well, never mind! Another enjoyable afternoon was almost over. Henry resisted the temptation to cast again, in that place anyway. But there were a couple of casts still to come and daylight would not last for ever. He smirked and suppressed a tiny stab of conscience as he took a long look downriver, moving his gaze slowly out of the patch of weedy slack water where he'd spent the last hour: over a wide band of sluggish current that swept towards the Plattsford Road Bridge carrying the main Plattsford/Wiscliffe Road over the river; through the first main arch whose shadows darkened the water to jade; past a line of thick clumps of river-trailing reeds and onwards to the sail-bristled shore of Wiscliffe Yachting Marina and Caravan Club, where thirty assorted craft bobbed at the fringe of the river.

Down there, lay his little bit of poaching.

Laying his rod athwart the gunnels, Henry rose to his feet, braced himself against the sudden rocking motion of the punt and lifted his dripping keep-net from the water, revealing its wriggling contents. He had about six pounds of mixed small stuff, roach mainly, with one or two bleak and gudgeon and a nice tench around the pound mark. By no means a bad session. This had turned out to be quite a productive little backwater and it was a pity he hadn't found it sooner, but now that he had, he could look forward to some more good catches.

After a long, admiring look at the mixed bag, he upended the net and slid the fish back into their native element. Then he shook the drips from the net, folded it, laid it in the well of the punt and went to work on his rod.

Off with the centre-pin reel and gossamer-thin line. On instead with the Mitchell thread-line job, bearing its load of five-pound-breaking-strain monofilament. No float or lead weight this time, but just a big ringed hook — size four — tied directly to the line. He lodged the assembled hook under the reel-fitting, tightened up and was ready to move off.

The anchor — a large stone at the end of a rope — yielded easily and as the punt began to drift slowly towards the main current Henry picked up his single paddle and, redskin-fashion, propelled the craft gently downstream.

Fifty yards brought him close to the bridge, close enough to read the prominent black-and-yellow notice plugged to the stonework. He had read the notice many times and knew its contents verbatim, but he never passed by that spot without reading it again:

'WISCLIFFE HERON
ANGLING CLUB.
END OF CLUB WATERS.
NO FISHING
BEYOND THIS POINT.'

What a silly, misleading notice it was, to be sure. 'No Fishing ALLOWED . . . ' would have been a precise and accurate message, but 'No Fishing' was nonsense. Because there was some excellent fishing beyond this point, and Henry knew exactly where to find it. His membership of the Wiscliffe Heron Club gave him no rights there, that was true enough, and Henry had no other permission from whoever *did* own the rights. But the water always fished well and that made it worth the risk. Henry had been poaching there regularly for some years, taut-nerved always, ultra-timorous under the stress of his own deliberate trespass but excited as a schoolboy embarking on fresh adventure. The recurring escapade was his private ritual of derring-do.

The notice drifted by overhead and Henry forgot about it, to concentrate instead on the approach to his little secret pool. Immediately below the bridge he shipped his paddle and sat unmoving as the punt made its slow, smooth progress downstream: across the green water laced with patterns of reflection from bankside foliage; past the ramshackle stone structure set back from the river which had four mouldering walls and a sagging roof and which Henry had long since named 'The Fortress'; alongside the deeper hued green of the great bed of tall-fronded reeds and onwards to the very mouth of the pool.

He fixed his eyes on the passing scene and — suddenly — there it was, dark and mysterious, overhung with grass and trailing reeds, a trickle of spring-water marbling its surface at the far end and the resultant shift of rolling current quite discernible as it swirled on its way to join the main river.

Lake Ceylon.

Henry had named it so from the first. As a reluctant schoolboy he had once sweated over a project on Ceylon and had carefully mapped its outline. He knew that the curious dew-drop shaped territory was not a lake, but an island. And yet the small secluded pool matched the larger Eastern Country remarkably well for shape, and the naming had been so natural, so *right*. No bigger than a cafe-awning, Lake Ceylon seemed insignificant, but to Henry's certain knowledge it was home to a thriving colony of plump and greedy chub, some of them bigger fish than he had ever seen out of water.

Sometimes, when he drifted silently past the pool like this, he could actually see the shoal, but tonight the Wissey was carrying a touch of colour and he could only imagine them lying there, heads to spring's runnel, like a flotilla of ships.

Thirty yards downstream of the pool he leaned over the edge of the punt, grasped a clump of reeds and held tightly until the punt swung nose-in to the bank and grounded on the bankside reeds with a slithering jolt. Then, with his rod balanced in one hand and holding the mooring rope with the other he crept stealthily ashore. Once on solid ground, he heaved the punt's prow till it rested high on springy rushes. Then he made fast by knotting the mooring rope to a thick bunch of the same plant.

Reaching into the punt for his landing-net and haversack he festooned the tackle about his body and began to creep along the river bank, heading

19

upstream. When he came to the well-recognised patch of trodden ground just below Lake Ceylon he settled, half-crouching, hardly daring to breathe.

Unfastening the side pocket of the haversack he fumbled in its depths and took out a small, plastic box. Inside the box there was a layer of thickly matted dock-leaves and he lifted the layer aside. There they were, clinging to the base of the box like limpets on a rock. Two fat, black, shiny garden slugs. Beautiful! Beautiful!

Strange how so many people — particularly members of the angling fraternity who ought to know better — were repelled by these sticky, harmless creatures and would never bait with them at any price. Thank God the chub had no such scruples. To them, slugs were bounty — the food of heaven — like chunks of treacle toffee falling from the sky.

Baiting with a single slug Henry gauged the distance to the tiny, twinkling pool and swung the baited tackle outwards. Good shot! The slug fell with a loud plop, stirring a bright ring at the neck of the pool. And the response was electric. Instantly, magically, the line shot away taut as a gallus-band and Henry struck firmly. But there was no resistance. The rod arched rearward and the bare hook came whistling back to lodge in the rank grass tussocks at his side. The ripples on the pool's surface widened and grew less.

A damned good bite, that. But he'd failed to make contact and some greedy old chub had retired into the depths to munch on a prime morsel, unaware, perhaps, that only providence had prevented its undignified exit from the water.

Just one slug left. One more chance. Once again he swung, not so accurately this time, but at least the slug had landed in the pool and there was an instantaneous take. This time luck favoured Henry and the short rod arched till it seemed it must surely break. But it stood firm against the strain and Henry rejoiced to the feel of a tugging, diving chub.

This was one of the giant fellows, he could tell that by the feel of him. Much bigger, he seemed, than any Henry had caught previously. But no. As the fish succumbed and its struggles abated he knew he had been mistaken. It was a nice fish, but not one of the monsters that Lake Ceylon surely held. Two and a half pounds he estimated as he slid his net under the gasping fish and gently drew it ashore.

3

IT was a perfect end to the day.

Over the years, Henry Crumble-stone had seen many thousands of fish gleaming and gulping in his hands, but he never ceased to wonder at their beauty. *Thanks for a brave tussle old chap*, he said silently as he admired the sleek silver belly, the olive brown back and the gleam of fiery bronze along the flanks. *And now be off with you, and grow a pound or two before you call on me again.*

He slid the chub gently back into the water, pointed its head upstream and grinned happily as it flicked its tail and sped away. The last and best fish of the day was gone amid subsiding ripples, but there were many specimens like that in Lake Ceylon and he'd be . . .

"Hey! You!"

The voice startled Henry. It came from very close behind him and its ringing tones reverberated in his ears like a clap of thunder. Rising to his feet and turning, he beheld a fearful mountain of a man wearing a white roll-neck sweater, white trousers and wellington-boots turned over at their tops. The man was hugely framed and tending to fatness and his round, bulging face was scarlet with rage. Henry had never stood so close to him before, but he knew the man well enough by sight and by repute. This was Basil Jenks who, as its President, ruled the Wiscliffe Yachting Marina and Caravan Club with the force of a despot. Jenks was an all too familiar figure in Wiscliffe Society. He was central to many local disputes and his fame as a mischief-maker was legendary.

Henry blinked up at him, timidly.

"You're Crumblestone, the Solicitor, aren't you?" Jenks said pompously.

"Yes," Henry acknowledged mildly.

"Well, you're trespassing. This is private land."

"I'm very sorry, I . . . "

Henry flushed guiltily as he realised he had very nearly told a lie. The words of denial had hovered, part-formed, on his lips: — *'I didn't know it was private'*. But in fact he knew quite well that he had no right to be standing on that strip of land. Till now, he hadn't known for certain who the owners were. The short length of river bank adjoined the Marina on its upstream side. On almost every weekend in the summer he'd seen it thronged with boating-types in their shorts, 'T' shirts and peaked caps and, although the Club's moorings were well downstream and on the far side of their entrance channel, he still should have suspected that they owned this land also.

So he couldn't honestly plead ignorance. Jenks was showing more animosity than was strictly called for, but the rights and wrongs of the situation were plain. Jenks was right and Henry wrong.

" . . . I was just going," he finished stupidly.

"Be quick about it then," Basil Jenks snapped. "You've no right to come traipsing over somebody else's land — and this is not the first time. I've had it reported that you've been before. I've a damned good mind to send for the police and make an example of you. If I catch you here again, that's what I shall certainly do. Now clear off, or there'll be trouble — and don't let me have to tell you again."

There was no kind of response which would meet the case. Humbly and wordlessly, Henry gathered his tackle together and slunk away, skirting Jenks and heading for the punt.

The punt was no longer where he had left it.

Henry's heart missed a beat and he looked wildly about him, unable to accept the evidence of his eyes. And then he saw the punt. It was a few yards downriver, clear of the bankside reeds and drifting slowly away. He hurried in its wake, hoping to reach it from some other point, but it stayed tantalisingly out of reach. Worse than that, in a very few seconds it would drift into the wide mouth of the Marina's entrance channel and onwards to the main current, where it might be lost for ever.

Better by far if it had been Henry's own property, for then there would only have been personal loss, but unfortunately it belonged to the Wiscliffe Heron Angling Club and they'd never forgive him if he lost one of their punts, particularly if it happened during a blatant poaching session. Poaching was an activity which that well-ordered and rule-abiding Club would never tolerate.

But there might still be a chance.

Henry unshipped his line and cast wildly in the direction of the punt, missed it by a yard and lost valuable time as he wrenched his hook free of tangling reeds. *Time for one more cast. Careful with the flighting now, and give it everything you've got.* This time, the line fell across the thwarts and he heard the hook tinkle against a seat bracket. In an agony of hope and doubt he tightened the line. Thank God! The hook seemed to have found purchase and slowly, ever so carefully, Henry was able to swing the punt to the shore.

Basil Jenks was standing right behind him. He had watched the whole proceedings, face bright with malice and amusement. Now he guffawed.

"Maybe that'll teach you to tie up properly in future," he sneered, "only next time make damned sure you don't moor to our land — and that includes the whole banking. Now clear off and don't ever let me catch you here again. If I do, I'll give you bloody Crumblestone," he paused and laughed at his own unspoken joke, then added: — "I'll have you crumbling rocks my friend. On Dartmoor."

★ ★ ★

Shamed beyond endurance, Henry stowed his gear and clambered aboard the punt, shoving off into open water. He shook his head ruefully, unable to believe he could have been so careless as to almost lose the punt. But of course he hadn't been careless at all. When he thought about it, he remembered quite clearly that he had made the mooring rope very secure.

The rope was still trailing in the water over the prow and Henry shipped his paddle, leaned over and retrieved it, drawing its dripping length aboard. A large sheaf of dark green reeds was still firmly knotted to the business end — too large a sheaf to have broken easily.

He examined the reeds.

At one end they tailed off into a dripping, narrowing spike, but at the other end they were of precisely equal length, which was not particularly surprising.

Quite obviously, they had been cut with a sharp knife.

That swine Jenks had cut the punt free.

But that couldn't really be what had happened, Henry decided after the first sharp stab of anger. Jenks had tongue-lashed him for several minutes, and all that time he'd been standing quite close to Henry, well within his view.

If Jenks had cut the punt free it must have been *before* then, in which case the punt would surely have drifted out of sight. So the cutting must have taken place *during* the delivery of Jenks' spiteful lecture — and clearly by somebody else.

Jenks had an accomplice as mean and cruel as himself.

* * *

The truth was inescapable and it saddened Henry, but another thought bugged him as he drove slowly homeward that evening. Jenks had known him by name and profession.

'You're Crumblestone, the Solicitor, aren't you?'

An innocent enough question to be sure, but it puzzled Henry that Jenks should have had that knowledge. As far as he knew, his firm had had no dealings with Jenks, certainly none in which Henry had personally figured, nor had he ever met the man socially. It seemed unlikely that Jenks would ever have heard of him — yet there was little doubt he had.

And Henry wondered how — and when — and from whom.

4

HE was still pondering the problem next day when he arrived at the offices of Messrs Cantwell Grace and Tomlinson, a Firm of Solicitors with whom he was a junior partner. No answer had suggested itself.

Henry was listless and completely out of sorts. He was not generally an idler, but for once he ignored the modest pile of papers in his 'In' tray and after bidding his secretary a formal 'Good-morning' he sat at his desk, frowning and twisting paper-clips to destruction.

There was always plenty for Mary Dawkins to do at the start of a working day and because she was engrossed in her work in her own little cubby-hole she noticed nothing amiss.

At mid-morning, Mary spooned

coffee-powder into her own cup and Mr Crumblestone's large decorated beaker, humming quietly to herself as she waited for the kettle to boil. This was a daily ritual and she enjoyed it. To her, it was a labour of love. Mr Crumblestone was always so appreciative and that made working for him a pleasure.

Until her appointment as his private secretary more than four years earlier, her small, dapper and most agreeable boss had always taken his morning coffee and afternoon tea from the Company trolley which trundled down the corridor twice daily, bearing its cauldron-brew from the canteen. But Mary had soon put a stop to that. She had donated a small kettle which, together with a tray of cups and spoons bought with petty cash, now lived permanently in the cupboard behind her typing chair. So their small working unit was self-sufficient. Mr Crumblestone drank freshly made beverages whenever it suited him and coffee at ten was an essential service, more important to Mary than all the rest of the work of the small office.

At twenty-nine, Mary Dawkins was beyond the first bloom and silliness of youth. A tall, willowy girl with impeccable dress-sense and a strong will, she had an abundance of womanly regard for the comfort of her charge, who happened to be Mr Crumblestone. She lived her role as earnestly as she would have doted on the husband she had never had.

No sublimated spinster she. Her single state was not of her own choosing but rather the failure of her stars. There had been three young men in her life: Peter, for whom she would have made any sacrifice but who had left her tearful and bereft after kindly but awkwardly announcing that he loved another; Geoffrey, who had looked for sacrifices too quickly and had dismissed her with foul abuse when they were not forthcoming; and gentle George, who probably still loved her and yearned after her, but whose rather too childish admiration had roused no answering chords in Mary Dawkins.

She had tried hard to love George, because there was no comfort in her tiny bachelor home and no status in living alone, but the simple need for a husband had been insufficient of itself to cleave her to George and, recognising that truth, she had firmly repulsed him.

Mary had few regrets about the past, but the ones she had, all concerned George. Peter she still admired, but he had married successfully and produced his brood of happy children, and who could regret that? Her memory of Geoffrey was a well-healed wound, licked briefly and dismissed as one of life's lessons.

If only there had not already been a Mrs Henry Crumblestone?

Mary rattled spoon on saucer as she angrily suppressed that most improper thought. But there was no use pretending it never came to her, indeed it had recurred incessantly since she had first come to work for this kindly man, but there was something immodest in even *thinking* that way about someone who was happily married. Mr Crumblestone was such a nice, dignified, responsible person, and there could be no honesty in meddling, even mentally, with his private life.

Besides, there was more to happiness than mere domesticity. The ordinary relationships of business brought their own brand of comradeship and she had that in full measure. Mr Crumblestone was a delight to work for. There was no oppressiveness in his make-up, no tantrums or temper. Always a polite request for her assistance when he might have demanded it of her and always a grateful 'thank-you' for each task performed, when the tasks were no more than her bounden duty. Best of all, he talked to her.

And those conversations alone were reward enough.

In the early days of their relationship

he had been reticent, almost secretive, but the cause had been a barrier of shyness, easy to overcome. Nowadays they knew each other so well that he was much more free with his confidences. It shamed Mary, sometimes, to realise how much trust he placed in her and how much detail he passed on to her of matters which ought properly to be classed as personal. To honour his confidences was a crusade. She would never ever let him down.

The kettle mouthed steam and she scalded the coffee, stirring rapidly to dissolve the sugar before cooling-off with milk. The clock on his office wall showed half a minute short of ten as she carried the loaded tray to his desk, slid the saucer of cream biscuits in front of him and set the beaker down carefully on a clean beer-mat.

"There you are, Mr Crumblestone."

"Thank you, Miss Dawkins."

It was exactly the same response as usual, but it sounded wrong, very wrong. She could hardly fail then, to be aware of his preoccupation. He had responded with a start — guiltily — and the customary smile was absent. She felt a stab of worry.

In truth, Henry was still brooding about the events of the night before. Not the fishing, or any of the pleasures of those hours on the river, but his clash with the coarse-mouthed Jenks and its disagreeable outcome.

He deplored the other's inhumanity even more than he despised himself for having provoked it. The bad-tempered wigging delivered by Jenks had been an unnecessary humiliation, even though Henry had richly deserved some admonishment. He could have found room in his heart to forgive such boorishness if the thing had ended there.

But it had not ended there.

The shabby trick of deliberately cutting the punt adrift had been the act of a blackguard, and a dangerous one. A man capable of doing a thing like that would stoop to anything. And even though Jenks had not personally done the deed, his unknown accomplice had, and Jenks knew all about it. With a bit of quick thinking and quicker action, Henry had saved the day, but if luck had not been with him the punt might easily have been lost — and the ramifications of that were too serious to contemplate.

Yet in the depths of his heart it was none of those things that troubled Henry most. The truly shattering misfortune was the aftermath. He had been dispossessed of a loved facility. As the respectable and right-thinking man he was, Henry knew very well that he could never again trespass in that quiet little spot. His intrusions had harmed no-one, he felt sure, but he had been ordered off and there was no need for twice-telling. Lake Ceylon was closed to him. There would be no more opportunity of pursuing those handsome chub in their softly sheltered home, and that was a tragedy past bearing.

Awakening to the arrival of Mary Dawkins with his coffee he tried hard to conceal his dolour, but his wan face and troubled eyes were all too revealing.

"You haven't done a thing, Mr Crumblestone," she accused.

"What's that? Oh yes, I see. Still, I've only got a few letters to sign, and they can wait."

"Drink your coffee and tell me what's the matter."

"The matter? Nothing!" he lied.

"But what's troubling you, Mr Crumblestone? Because something is. You can't hide it from me."

And at that, he realised he could hide his troubles from nobody. Looking up at her, he saw at once a way of easing his own burden. *Dear Miss Dawkins. She was smiling broadly, as usual, daring him to be miserable in her presence. What a happy and cheerful girl she was, to be sure. Her homely manner was a breath of spring sunshine on even the darkest day. He had always been able to talk to Mary. He would talk to Mary now.*

He told her about the night before and she listened.

"Poor Mr Crumblestone!" she said.

5

BUT Mary also said a great deal more. She filled his ears with a flood of wise words, a symphony of warmth, understanding and consolation.

And in the depths of coffee and the comfort of Mary's sympathy, Henry pushed the painful incident on the river from his mind — hardly thought about it again, in fact, for almost a week.

It was on the following Friday evening, as he steered his two-year-old Rover towards the suburban detached house where he lived, that he remembered most vividly. The week-end lay before him, and this was the first week-end for years when he would have to forego his little bit of poaching. A wise philosopher might have been less perturbed than Henry was. The Wissey was a fine river, well blessed with other places to go in search of chub. The Wiscliffe Heron Club held rights over almost three miles of very good, varied water, and Henry was fully entitled to fish the whole of it. But sadly, that was not enough. Nowhere else in the district was there a spot so promising or so tantalising as the little secret Lake Ceylon.

With a sensation of deep loss, he reminded himself that although it was barred to him he would always be able to see, if not the forbidden spot, at least the rushes where it lay concealed. And much as it would irk him to see, the vision would draw him like a magnet.

Impulsively, he detoured and headed out on the Plattsford Road. As he approached the bridge he turned into a shallow natural lay-by, stopped, climbed out of his car and walked out on the bridge, consciously hugging the parapet on the upstream side. Yonder, stretching beyond the limit of his vision, lay the lower reaches of the Wiscliffe Heron Club water.

It was an attractive stretch with plenty of character, with deeps and shallows, fasts and slacks, weedy jungles and limpid clear pools. Reedy banks stood cool and green on either hand, while here and there a willow trailed its lissome branches over the darkened water.

Good fishing, all of it, with fine specimens resident everywhere. For ten years now, Henry had been privileged to spend all the time he wanted there, bank-walking or afloat on that lush river, a fully paid-up member of the club. The custom-built Club Headquarters with its stout jetty and half-dozen communal punts was out of sight upstream, round the far bend. But Henry could see it in his mind's eye, and what a convenient, well-appointed headquarters it was.

As Henry knew, Club water ended at this point.

Somewhere beneath him — out of sight unless he breasted the parapet and peered dangerously down — was the painted sign which proclaimed the downstream limits of his entitlement. Often enough in the past, he'd ignored that sign and ventured into the forbidden territory below the bridge. But henceforward, he reminded himself sadly, there would be no ignoring the sign, for the unfished water was doubly out of bounds.

He had only come there to torture himself.

Turning, he stood with his shoulders braced against the parapet and, when there was a lull in passing traffic, he hurried across the carriageway to lean against the opposing parapet and gaze ruefully downstream. Lake Ceylon was not visible, but its setting of dark green reeds was in plain view and Henry's heart sank as he cast his eye over their tossing heads. There was a wild beauty in that scene — a beauty that had once been his to enjoy, but was his no longer.

It hurt Henry like physical pain to see the beauty. He resolved that he would not stand at that spot ever again. This would be his last look. After all, if the sweet-shop was closed there was no profit in pressing an eager nose to its window. Jenks had denied him the chance of fishing there, so he would forget that the place existed.

If it proved possible to forget.

Henry Crumblestone would have gone away then, in accordance with his vow, but something unfamiliar and out of place imposed itself on his eye. It was something white and chunky, lying a little way inland from the river, on the far side of the dark expanse of reeds and half-obscured by the crumbling walls of the old stone building he called The Fortress. By peering closely he identified what he saw.

New fencing material!

Concrete posts piled loosely in a heap like spent matches, rolls of green chain-link mesh and pineapple coils of gleaming barbed wire.

So Jenks and his cronies meant business. Henry's small intrusion into their preserve must have made the proprietors of the Wiscliffe Yachting Marina more incensed than he had imagined. They'd had their fill of trespassers, it seemed, and they intended to have no more. They proposed to erect a substantial fence completely around their property. It would serve to repel all intruders of course, but Henry had the feeling that they were doing it specifically for him.

He groaned aloud. This was absolute folly. His own conscience would have been fence enough and such an elaborate barrier was quite unnecessary. To make matters worse, a wire and concrete fence along that unspoiled bank would create an eyesore to end eyesores. It would turn a beautiful piece of river into a spiky jungle, a lush, natural setting into something resembling a zoo.

Henry's lip drooped petulantly and he scourged himself for having been the unwitting cause of such an ecological disaster. How big a scar, he wondered, did they intend to carve on the face of the countryside? He looked afield.

Further back towards the sweep of the main road they had already begun to erect the fence. Five tall posts with angled tops stood in military line, ranging down the slope of the road's embankment, diagonally towards the river.

But diagonally *downstream*.

They were well off course, surely? If the fence continued in the direction it was going it would miss the bed of reeds completely. Yet, clearly, that must be their intention. Why else would they begin fencing as they had?

Perhaps it had something to do with the consistency of the ground? Henry had never looked closely at the terrain beyond and behind Lake Ceylon, but he looked now, and the overall colour he saw was dark green. It was reedy, marshy land all right. Unsuitable, very likely, for erecting fence posts except in selected places. The Marina people must have realised the fact, and they were going to cut their losses by skirting the reed bed completely.

But had they seen the consequence of that? If they advanced too close to the river before fencing upstream to the bridge they would cut their monstrous swathe right through the heart of Lake Ceylon, hammering great concrete pillars into that serene little sea and driving the residents away in panic — perhaps never to return.

Ah well! It would make little difference to Henry. Let them choose whichever path they might, he was banned the area. If it suited the Wiscliffe Yachting Marina and Caravan Club to plaster expensive wire and concrete all over the place, that was their own business.

★ ★ ★

Three evenings later, Henry Crumblestone stood once more at the same spot. He had been determined not to return, but curiosity had waged war with determination and emerged the winner.

This time the scene was much changed and he stared in wonder and bewilderment. Work had evidently gone on right through the week-end and the gleaming length of fence was complete. The massed diamonds of green mesh ran taut from pole to pole and the whole was topped with five strands of silvery wire with scintillating barbs. It presented a daunting barrier to all but the most daring.

But a barrier from what?

The new fence ran arrow straight from road to river. It was true that the strip of river bank from which Jenks had so rudely ordered him away was enclosed within the new fence. Indeed, the last few posts marched right down and into the very water's edge at the upstream end of that strip of disputed territory. But the bed of waving reeds was *not* contained, nor indeed — so far as Henry could tell when looking from the bridge — was the spot where Lake Ceylon lay.

What, then, about the broad wedge of territory standing *outside* the fence on its upstream side?

Feeling a tiny prickle of curiosity, Henry looked to his left along the bridge parapet and followed with his eyes the edge of the main road until that line met the start of the new fence at something less than a right-angle.

That was the apex.

Diverging from that point, fence and bridge formed the two sides of a roughly equilateral triangle whose base was the river itself. The whole of the reed-bed, the strip of lush bank right up to the footstones of the bridge and — most important of all — Henry's secret Lake Ceylon, were all contained in that thickly overgrown triangle of land.

By the posting of their notice on the bridge, the Wiscliffe Heron Angling Club had unequivocally proclaimed the *downstream* limit of their interest. The Wiscliffe Yachting Marina and Caravan

Club had likewise staked its claim — and done so with the most precise delineation. Their fence marked the *upstream* boundary of the land they said was theirs.

Two boundaries.

Mutually exclusive, but not conterminous.

Between the two, there remained a juicy chunk of real-estate to which nobody — overtly at least — had avowed their right.

No Man's Land????

6

HIS curiosity now hotly aroused, Henry set out to walk the bounds of his discovery.

He walked off the bridge and followed the line of the road until he came to the first post of the new fence. He saw at once that it had been built to form an angle with an already existing but lower chain-link fence that divided the Marina's land from the main road. New strands of barbed wire had been used to make an intermingled joint and seal off the weak juncture between the two. The old fence was heavily overgrown with thorn and bramble twined about with nettles and willow-herb, which explained why Henry had never noticed it before.

But the box-angle formed by new fence and old, stood quite separate from the first stonework of the bridge parapet. There was an intervening gap of perhaps eight feet, which was superficially hedged by a line of spindly hawthorn saplings, their branches choked with ferns.

It was a natural gateway. Remove those scraggy bushes, grub them out and tamp their sockets, and an entrance would be revealed opening directly onto the triangle of reedy land which stretched from that point down to the river. There was even a run-off from the road, right alongside the gap, where the tar-macadam surface ended and the footway along the bridge parapet had not yet begun.

A man might easily have established a little haven there, a holding, quiet and secluded, sandwiched between the two established holdings to left and right.

But could there be anything worth husbanding?

It seemed strange that the land within the triangle should be so obviously untrodden. Even if nobody else cared, hundreds of anglers fished the river in those parts and surely some of them must have considered the little plot at the bridge corner as a likely avenue of approach? There were, as Henry knew, many easier points of access to the river, but surely *somebody* would have been venturous enough to blaze a new trail at that point? Yet nobody had done so.

If, indeed, enough firm ground existed.

The explanation must lie in the look of the place. Henry had to admit it might be off-putting. The first feature to hit the eye was the deep olive-green colour that suffused the whole triangle, making the ground look treacherous — unsafe. Indeed, the place probably *was* treacherous and unsafe. Just a wasted piece of unusable bog.

But there was sixty yards of river, and there was Lake Ceylon. That much he knew. Henry felt suddenly as Darwin must have felt before venturing ashore in search of strange lands. In the circumstances, Henry could hardly do less. So he straddled the stunted bushes, swung himself across and set off on a tentative voyage of discovery.

Moving slowly riverwards in a direct line from the road, he tested each foothold in advance before transferring his weight. For fifteen paces the ground felt springy and firm, but the sixteenth pace deceived him and he felt water seeping into his brogue. Hastily he took another step and found firm ground again. So the first bit of marshiness had been no more than a runnel, a moisture-holding wrinkle in the ground.

He angled slightly towards the downriver corner where lay his secret pool, and for a few more paces it seemed he would reach the pool without trouble. But just as he was gaining confidence his leading foot thrust through a layer of moss and his shiny brogue disappeared into a pit of slime and water.

He drew the foot back with difficulty and halted, teetering as he looked ahead. A twenty yard band of thick green rushes lay between him and Lake Ceylon — thirty yards of the same between him and the river bank itself. Impossible to fish either pool or river from that point.

Unless??

It occurred to Henry that the obstacle was not so much distance as the physical barrier of growing plants. Of course, if the whole area proved to be as marshy as the patch right in front of him, there was no way he could cross it without infilling or draining off. But there might be firmer ground concealed by the rushes — and rushes could always be chopped out. With a bit of sensible pruning he might be able to clear enough of the growth to make access to the river from this point a practical proposition.

And then he decided to leave them for the time being.

Because his eyes had roved elsewhere. He had seen the broken down stone structure which stood well to his right and nearer the bridge, and the thought had come to him that *no matter what* the building had been used for, there had to be some access to it. If not now, then at some time in the past. Nobody ever put stone on stone except at a reachable spot.

Retracing his steps until he came to firm ground again, Henry took off at a tangent, upstream this time, heading for the old building. He needed to pick his way carefully. By the time he reached the front of the building his left foot was squelching and both trouser-legs were mud stained as far as the knees.

But he was there — he had arrived — and the deepest marsh he had encountered along the way had been no more than a foot or so in depth. Having made the journey once he could easily do so again, especially if he came properly kitted-out with old trousers and wellington-boots.

The building was bigger than it had seemed from the river, but it was a very simply designed box-like structure and Henry doubted if it had ever been used as a dwelling. The walls were of rough stone, and if there had been mortar filling the cracks it was there no longer. Surprisingly, though, there was nothing like so much damage to the walls as there had seemed from a distance.

The windows — of which three out of the four walls had one — were mere rectangular cavities in the stonework, innocent of frame or glazing. One of the window-holes, on the side overlooking the river, had lost its upper sill and part of one edge had crumbled. That, he recognised, was what had given the place its dilapidated look. That — and the roof, which was composed of heavy stone tiles supported on wooden struts, or rather, only partly supported, for the roof bellied inwards alarmingly over most of the central area.

There was no chimney, and no sign that the building had ever been furnished with one.

There was a ricketty wooden door of strut-and-plank design hanging on one hinge over the entrance. Henry opened it and went inside. He found himself standing in a rectangular room which was the whole of the interior. The only way in or out was the door by which he had entered. It was light and there was no musty smell. The floor was of earth, hard-packed round the four sides but damp and soft in the central area where rain had entered through the roof. There was a tracery of scuffs and scratches in the soft soil — animal or bird tracks no doubt — but no sign of a human footprint other than his own.

The absence of human signs affected Henry in a curious way. He felt as though he had intruded upon a fairy spot from which all human creatures were excluded. And yet, humans had certainly built the place. As a store-room or an animal shed perhaps? Whatever its original purpose, it did not seem to have been used for ages.

Perhaps it really was a martial relic,

from the last — or some earlier — war? In a sense it had the appearance of a modern day pill-box or guard post, with gun-slits facing forwards and to each side. That was why he had christened it The Fortress. Was it possible that he had guessed correctly? Henry knew it was a ridiculous fancy, but it pleased him and he was chuckling as he headed for the door.

There was a great deal more to see yet.

Leaving The Fortress he circled to his right and found himself no more than twenty paces from the river. He moved in that direction and immediately lost his footing and fell to his knees. The intervening ground which had appeared to be fairly level, actually fell away towards the river bank. The Fortress, he realised, had been built atop a hump of ground — deliberately — as a safeguard against too much flooding, but due to the dense cloak of spreading vegetation that fact had not been apparent until now.

Henry picked his way down the slope, pressing a path through tall weeds, till he stood beside the waters of the Wissey. The ground underfoot felt good and solid. A bit of scrub-clearing would soon transform this spot into a first class vantage from which to fish the river. Always supposing that the quality of fishing hereabouts was such that the trip would be worthwhile.

To check, he stood on tip-toe and bending forward over the riverside reeds he peered at the water immediately below the bridge at the point where the first arch soared upwards in its span. Aboard his punt he had floated over the water there times without number, but from the bank the water looked utterly different — more attractive somehow.

The main current swirled well away from that first arch and such movement as there was in the water was sluggish. In the shadow of the bridge the river was green and opaque — sure signs of depth — and wherever there was depth there would surely be abundant shoals of fish.

Moving away from the bridge, Henry began to pace slowly downstream, parallel with the river, prodding forward with his feet. The bank still seemed firm enough. It would have to be well-knitted of course, otherwise the swirling brown water of spate which was a common feature of the River Wissey would have eroded the soil long before.

From time to time he leaned over the reeds to examine the river. The green deeps seemed to continue, though the reed bed itself began to thicken perceptibly until it became virtually impassable. Several yards short of the edge of his secret pool, Henry was obliged to stop, or risk stepping amid a jungle of matted vegetation which, for anything he knew, might have no solid base.

But he was nearer than had once seemed possible. In fact the far edge of Lake Ceylon was tantalisingly within view, so close that if he had held an assembled rod at that time he would have risked a cast to reach the water. So there was golden promise here. Some careful reed-cutting might place him even nearer. It began to look as though the pool was not lost to him — Jenks or no Jenks.

Turning, he surveyed the whole of the wedge of land. So far he had trodden only a small part of its surface but what he had discovered filled him with hope. At a cautious estimate the land must measure half an acre — and it was usable land, all of it.

There was good fishing here, and it was quiet and sheltered, if rather too abundantly blessed with plant life. Nobody, it seemed certain now, had exploited the land or the fishing within recent times, but it was there to be exploited. And above all, nobody seemed to be pressing claim to ownership of the land.

Untrodden land? Unregistered territory? Land free for the taking? A garden, untamed and uncultivated?

These were intriguing questions and Henry Crumblestone was pleasantly thoughtful as he picked his way back to his car and started for home.

Was this an opportunity to be grasped?

His smattering of knowledge of the Law of Real Property — remembered from his student days and unpractised since then — told him that he could make a limited use of it, at least until its owner dispossessed him.

And if there should be no dispossession? Well, twelve years use, uninterrupted, would give him Adverse Title. Not that he dared to hope such a long limitation period would ever be allowed to run its course. He might last a fortnight — a month even — and after that he could expect to be discovered and turned off. And any work he did in that period, as well as any expense incurred, would be a total loss.

But even two weeks occupation in the scent of a young summer might repay a good deal of effort. And it might run to the full month — or even two months. The more Henry deliberated, the better the risk seemed.

Driving home, he freed his fancy to return and roam about the place he had just visited. It was a rough, dense and tangled place. But if the will were there and muscles would obey the will, it could be transformed into a place of green beauty.

A veritable Eden!

7

"HENRY CRUMBLESTONE! Take off those filthy shoes this minute. You've trodden mud all over my clean carpet."

Henry was already out of the house and heading towards the back garden, but the sound of his wife's voice pursued him. He winced at its sharp edge and glanced down at his feet. The brogues had dried out nicely after a few days against the heater in the shed, but the welts were still crammed with crumbly dried mud, so he could hardly deny her charge.

But really! Joan's fastidiousness was becoming quite unbearable lately. Houseproud to the point of mania, she had become so aggressive in her quest for tidiness that many a less mild husband would have taken to beating her soundly.

He smiled ruefully at the alien thought.

If there was one golden lesson he'd learned during those terrible years as a schoolboy, it was that Henry Crumblestone lacked the ability to beat anybody. It was not merely a matter of lack of will — though truthfully he rarely felt sufficiently angry to fight — it was a matter of physique.

'You're not big enough for this sort of thing, young Crumblestone,' his housemaster had once told him as he nursed a bloody nose after a flurry of fisticuffs with another pupil, *'so in future, you'd better pick on somebody half your size.'*

And Joan was every inch of twice his size.

She was an awe-inspiring example of the type usually described as statuesque. She had a good figure, but she was tall and stately beyond all reason, and alongside tiny Henry she seemed a giant of a woman.

Joan had been twice his size twelve

years earlier, when a short and awkward courtship had germinated into an uneasy but lawful alliance. Henry was never likely to forget their sweaty meeting on the rainbow floor of a Town discotheque, whither he had gone in desperation, seeking surcease from the ache of loneliness.

Joan had seen Henry coming a mile off and had latched on, showing him the way to glory in an utterly bewildering campaign to which he had had no defence. From shuffling his feet in the shadow of this tall and receptive stranger, to lying with pounding heart on the cushion of her ample bosom had seemed a lightning journey — and Joan had held the reins at every stage.

What was more, by God! He'd liked it.

Joan had made a man of Henry in a rapid burst of energy, and his own eager participation had exploded a host of myths about himself. He'd found pleasure in her flesh, as well as deep satisfaction in a rare sense of conquest that — for a brief while at any rate — had left him convinced of his own ability to dominate women.

That he could ever have dominated Joan, in any sense of the word, was a sick joke in retrospect, but just for once she had let him believe it. That they should afterwards marry — and without delay — had seemed the natural and laudable outcome of that wild night.

At the outset he had fancied himself in love with her, but that fancy fled more rapidly than it came. If there had been children, that would have altered the case, but nothing so wonderful had graced their union, and after the first twelve months she had let him know in unmistakable terms that not merely the potential fruiting but the seeding also, would be denied him.

For a short while after that, Henry still supposed that love — though unrequited — lived on within him, but now, twelve years on, he knew that the deeper emotion had never truly existed. He had been gulled into the tying of a knot and though the spell had faded, the knot remained.

It was not that Henry was displeased with marriage. He had discovered all kinds of advantages in possessing a wife that owed nothing to the bedroom. In return for those advantages he had learned to cope with a relationship that was in other respects unsatisfactory by bending to Joan's will, by being aloof, submissive, tolerant or evasive, as circumstances required.

He had even come to accept her undoubted infidelity.

At first, when he began to suspect that there really was another man in her life, Henry had refused to believe it. And Joan, for her part, had been commendably discreet, inventing all manner of excuses for frequent jaunts abroad coupled with late homecomings. But later on, she'd grown slack and uncaring, and from then on the signs had been easy to read and impossible to ignore.

The elaborate dressing-up in expensive

clothes for what were supposedly Church-meetings had been the first to become obvious. After that, a too liberal and highly uncharacteristic use of make-up and strong perfume, mild intoxication on a regular basis, the receipt of letters which she contrived to leave about her room and which, though he would not stoop to read them, spoke volumes, the unexplained telephone calls which — although she received them with a show of surreption and ended them with curious haste if Henry appeared on the scene — she made no real attempt to hide.

And finally, and most telling of all, the plastic card of contraceptive pills which lived openly on her dressing table and which Henry was not supposed to be able to recognise.

But Henry was not without vicarious sophistication. He knew their purpose very well, and he came to the only, and very obvious, conclusion. The truth interested him in a detached way, but by then he was so totally uninvolved with Joan that he hardly cared.

And now, he could smile, when she rated him over such a mild indiscretion as having dirty shoes.

★ ★ ★

Pretending not to have heard her peevish call, he scuttled along the crazy-paving of the garden path and passed among the tangle of rose bushes and creepers that flourished behind the house. At the far end of the garden he came to his shed-cum-workshop, a sanctuary which Joan never tried to invade, and passed inside, closing the door after him. The creosoted timbers sealed Henry off from the world and his wife and he forgot about Joan as he turned his attention to the much more captivating work in hand.

He had been engaged on the project for several evenings and the artistic bit was already done, the paint and varnish dry and hardening. Henry spent a moment or two admiring his handiwork before busying himself with saw, hammer and nails in putting the finishing touches to the job. He had been right to use new material and to be liberal with preservatives, for if everything went well his work would be exposed to all weathers for some time to come.

By mid-afternoon he was ready to load materials into his car and, not for the first time, he congratulated himself for having had the foresight to incorporate a second door at the rear of his roomy garage. The project was better kept from Joan, he had decided, and by sneaking round behind the roses he could pass from shed to garage unseen.

Some of the bulkier items would have to ride on the roofrack and would be in plain view when he drove away, but that would not happen until tomorrow, at crack of dawn, when Joan would still be asleep.

Tomorrow was Saturday, a recognised

fishing day. He could spend all of it by the river and Joan would see nothing at all unusual in that. Just so! But it would do no harm to pave the way. Before retiring that night, he reminded her:-

"Fishing tomorrow as usual, Joan, dear. I'll take a flask and sandwiches."

The information hardly registered.

Thank goodness she had never seen fit to oppose his hobby. Quite the contrary, she always seemed pleased to have him out of the house, where he could cause no mess. But she couldn't resist her usual admonishment which she delivered in ringing tones as he climbed the stairs.

"And make sure you scrub your feet before you come in."

Henry's mumbled "Yes, dear," was a small price to pay.

★ ★ ★

By seven o'clock next morning, wellington-booted and wearing his big quilted anorak against the morning chill, he was ready to leave. For the sake of appearances he took along his rods, nets and wicker-basket, and there was scarcely room for them in the boot.

Because Henry had no intention of going fishing.

As he drove light-heartedly in the direction of Plattsford Bridge he mentally ticked off the items he had smuggled from his shed and which were now distributed about the car. Spade and shears, timber and nails, hammer, wire, staples, hinges, padlock and hasp, a stout post sharpened at one end and — most valued of all — the rectangular notice which he had painted with loving care to a design that had caused him a deal of heart-searching. Knocking together the all-important notice had called for time and effort, but he felt sure he had got it right — exactly right. It would serve its purpose admirably.

It was perfect weather, warm and sunny with just a zephyr of cooling breeze. He parked alongside the gap between fence and bridge and for the rest of the day he worked and sweated, carrying, digging, hacking, chopping and nailing. When the work was done he stood back, mopped his brow and gazed in admiration at the picture he had created.

The bushes and herbage had all been cleared away from the gap, leaving a wide strip of newly dug and levelled soil. In place of the bushes stood a short section of wood and wire fencing which he had fashioned in his shed and brought to the spot ready made. It was Henry's very own fence.

Mid-way along the fence was a small gate, simply but neatly constructed from timber and wire-netting. 'T'-bar hinges held the gate to its stump and to secure it in position he had fitted a hasp and padlock, the key of which now reposed in his pocket. Thus he had provided a proper entrance to the triangle of land. It was an entrance and not a barrier. In no sense was it unscalable, but only Henry could properly use the gate.

But the *piece de resistance* was the notice. It stood proudly atop a robust wooden post, on the inside, a little way beyond the fence. The words on the notice were black on red and painted with his own hands. They were neat, legible and informative. In a burst of elation he read them aloud when there were no ears to listen.

'PRIVATE FISHING.
TRESPASSERS WILL BE
PROSECUTED.
BY ORDER.
HENRY V. CRUMBLESTONE.'

In the lower left hand corner, in much smaller lettering, he had added his address and telephone number. The details were difficult to read from outside the fence, but if anybody felt strongly enough about his impertinence to want to read them, they could always climb over.

And that was right.

For Henry's was no hole-in-the-corner invasion. If anyone on earth were to seek Henry V. Crumblestone, he had made sure they would know where to look.

He added the final touch almost as an afterthought.

It was a small strip of wood, bearing a single word in gilt lettering and carefully varnished over. Henry fixed it to the gate with a screw and it set the tone handsomely.

It was a lovely word.

'EDEN.'

Satisfied, he turned his back on Eden, but the scene lived on in his thoughts as he drove away. He had made a tangible announcement of his intentions and now he would wait three whole weeks before going back. Surely, in that time, trouble would have found him if it were ever to find him at all?

It was a brave notice he had erected for the world to see, especially the painted signature.

'HENRY V. CRUMBLESTONE.'

Henry had never been endowed with a middle name, but the intrusive 'V' seemed to give the whole legend a touch of authority.

Perhaps it stood for 'Vanity'?

8

SPRING was undergoing one of its unaccountable changes of mood. Henry had finished his work in the heat of a blazing sun, but the clouds were already massing unrealised on the horizon and as he drove away they came pressing in to blot out the day and turn the earth into a place of uninviting grey and misty dampness.

And the storm intensified.

Long before he drove into the streets of Wiscliffe the rain had begun to fall in earnest, its heavy drops bursting on the windscreen and drumming on the roof. He garaged the car and scuttled through the downpour to enter the house by the front door, ostentatiously scrubbing his shoes on the mat and earning the grudging approval of his wife.

The rain continued. By Sunday

morning it had increased to a steady downpour and the gutters of Wiscliffe ran with brown rivulets. Henry stayed indoors, to Joan's obvious annoyance, and by early afternoon he was prudently keeping out of her way. Promptly at three o'clock she donned her raincoat, gripped her umbrella and flounced out, *en route* so she told him to yet another meeting at the Church Hall. Henry was not displeased to see her go.

Minutes later — she could hardly have covered a hundred yards — a sharp rat-tat sounded on the front door and at first he supposed it was Joan returning. She must have forgotten her key or something. He hurried to the door, drew it open and stood gaping at the caller.

It was a policeman in uniform, his heavy storm-coat dripping water on the doorstep.

Henry was surprised and alarmed. Some unpleasant business was about to be enacted, there could be no doubt about that. And yet the constable looked cheerful enough, so perhaps there *was* a doubt? He speculated on the many possible reasons why the Constabulary might send its minion to his door. None seemed likely, but it was too early to assume bad news.

"Mr Crumblestone?" the constable enquired with a grin.

There was something a trifle worrying in his use of the name, but Henry saw no profit in renouncing his identity.

"Yes. I'm Crumblestone."

"So you own the piece of land by Plattsford Bridge?"

Oh dear God! Henry's body vibrated from shock and the constable was bound to have noticed the tremor. Henry looked about him wildly, hoping to find some other Mr Crumblestone on whom to lay the blame and for a panic spasm he contemplated a haughty rebuttal of the constable's accusation. But like a neon sign burning in his brain he could see plainly the small print on that damned revealing notice:-

'Prop. Henry V. Crumblestone.
    Primrose Cottage,
    9, Waverley Terrace,
    Grange Road Estate,
    Wiscliffe.'

Undeniably, this was the 'Primrose Cottage' alluded to, and he had already declared himself by acknowledging his name. So the game was up. It could only be a matter of seconds now before handcuffs were flourished and the constable did his duty. But the constable made no ominous move — he still seemed friendly — so Henry blurted a reply.

"Er, yes. Well, that is . . . "

"I thought so," the constable said affably. "That's what it said on the notice-board up there. I came here specially to see you, Mr Crumblestone. I wonder if you'd do us a big favour?"

"A favour? I don't see how I . . . "

The constable smiled more widely than ever. It was a frankly ingratiating smile and contained none of the hidden malice or half-concealed cruelty that Henry looked for.

"It's like this, you see, Mr Crumblestone. I'm P.C. Crossley, stationed here at Wiscliffe. I'm Secretary of the Constabulary Boating Section. We were out on the Wissey this morning and we had a little mishap."

"A mishap?"

"That's right. Nothing very serious. The river's well flooded by now, what with all this rain. We really shouldn't have risked it I suppose, but it's always easy to be clever after it's too late. We took our launch out for a run and, would you believe it, the engine conked. We couldn't get it started so we had to beach the boat."

"I'm afraid I still don't follow." But if Henry was puzzled by now, he was also filled with relief. This man in blue was no agent of an avenging Force with steel in his eyes and blood on his claws. He was a fellow-citizen and boat enthusiast who happened to be in some sort of trouble and had come in search of help.

"It's my fault for not explaining it too well," the constable confessed, "but I'm coming to it now. When the damned thing packed up, we dragged it ashore on your land. There was no alternative, you see. There was so much water coming down that we couldn't possibly have manhandled it upriver under the bridge. And by that time, there was hardly enough clearance anyway. We saw this nice little cut-back and . . . well . . . we heaved the boat in. We got pretty well drenched in the process," he said, ending on a wry note.

Henry was growing more relaxed all the time. By now he had recovered enough to smile in sympathy.

"I know the feeling," he said. "Accidents will happen, won't they? I mess about with boats a bit myself, and I know how tricky the floods can be. But you haven't said why you've come to see me. I think you mentioned something about a favour?"

"Yes. That's it. When we walked ashore we had to climb over your fence to get out. We knew it must be your fence because we saw your name on the notice."

"And you've damaged the fence?" Henry was faintly worried.

"Lord no! Nothing like that, Mr Crumblestone. We were particularly careful. But we had to leave the boat on your land, you see. There was nothing else to be done."

"Is that all?"

"All? Oh yes. Well, we'd like to leave it there till we've done a few repairs. I'm on afternoon duty this week. That's why I had to come here in uniform. But it means I can work on the engine in the morning. I can more or less promise to have it shifted by noon tomorrow."

Henry had the picture now and he beamed expansively.

"Think nothing of it, Constable,"

he said. "Leave it there as long as necessary. And if ever you need to use my place again, don't hesitate. Just take it as read."

Constable Crossley thanked him effusively and turned to go, leaving a cockahoop Henry Crumblestone beaming in his wake. Henry's mind was full of elated thought. He had occupied Eden for only a couple of days, but already there had been recognition, and from a most respectable source. It was as though the police had actively sponsored him, bringing him encouragement rather than the bad news he had feared.

From the constable's description, the Police Club's launch must have been punted in through a swollen Lake Ceylon and beached in the big reed-bed. The chub might not like that, but it was a temporary trouble, no more. It was the only course they could have taken. And yet . . .

"Just a minute, Constable," he shouted. The retreating figure stopped at the pavement and looked back enquiringly.

"Yes, sir?"

"I'm a teeny bit puzzled by one thing," Henry said. "There's a big Marina there, just below my place, with a wide entrance channel. I don't in the least mind having your launch, but I'd have thought the Marina would have been a much better place for mooring."

The constable grinned ruefully.

"So it would, sir, and that's a fact. But we've had dealings with that place before. Especially with the President, a chap called Basil Jenks. Do you happen to know the man?"

"Yes, we have some slight acquaintance," Henry admitted.

"Oh well, perhaps I shouldn't be saying this if he's a friend of yours. But really, you've no notion how unpleasant that man can be."

"Perhaps I have," Henry said. But he said it to himself.

★ ★ ★

Afterwards, Henry spent some time reviewing the exchange and its implications. A worthy man, Crossley. A man who could cross swords with Basil Jenks and emerge with such an accurate measure of his pedigree must be a valuable asset to the Force. But it was not Jenks and his universal pettiness that occupied Henry's mind. He effervesced with far happier thoughts.

He had listened to a policeman — by definition a shrewd and reliable person — who seemed to have accepted without question Henry's ownership of Eden.

'*Your fence*' '*Your notice-board*' '*YOUR LAND!*' The constable had said — and Henry himself had rounded the whole thing off by talking with firm authority of '*My place*'.

It seemed that the Patron Saint of soil and waterborne policemen was firmly on Henry's side.

★ ★ ★

And in the face of that, it hardly seemed to matter that the Patron Saint of marital fidelity was not.

It was still raining hard at the end of the day and he was in the house alone. Joan had returned briefly to serve him a salad tea and had then dolled herself up in finery and gone out again to yet another of her meetings.

In times long gone, Henry would have waited up for her, unable to settle till he knew she was back home, but such a thought had not crossed his mind in years. He was tired. He ate a frugal supper and retired early and, with no troubles to nag him, composed himself for sleep.

But golden prospects can be greater than worries as producers of insomnia. Henry slept but fitfully and woke in darkness, conscious that something had disturbed him. For a moment he lay on his back, staring at the ceiling and trying to identify the chugging sound that reached into his room. It was a motor vehicle of some sort, stationary but with its engine running. And by the sound of it, it was right in front of the house.

Even as he listened, the sound choked and ceased. Henry consulted his bedside alarm. It was half past two, a.m.

He rose, went to the window and peered out between the curtains. The pavements were still wet but the rain had stopped and the sky was clearing. As he'd thought, the car was parked right at his front gate. It was a Ford Granada in metallic silver, its sleek body glinting in the glow of the street lights. He had never seen it before as far as he knew, but then he had never had cause before to get up in the night and peer from his window in this way. From his angle of view it was impossible to see the occupants of the car, but he knew one of them for certain and the thought amused him.

His curiosity held him at the curtains

and he watched the car for several minutes, until Joan confirmed his suspicions by climbing out of the passenger side and waving as she tripped up the path to the house. The car started up and began to move off. Henry wondered who the driver could be.

The car had rolled only a yard or two. Its rear registration plate was well lit up and easy to read. Henry memorised the number and walked back to his bed, reciting the digits over in his mind. He took a spare visiting card and a ball-point pen from his wallet on the bedside table and, working in the glow from the street lights, inscribed the registration number on the card. He had no particular reason for doing so — was not even sure that he'd formed the letters and figures legibly — but having made the record he erased the memory and climbed back into bed, his curiosity allayed.

Joan could please her faithless self how she passed her time and with whom. He refused even to resent her conduct. For all he knew, half the street might have witnessed the event — and other events before it for that matter — but reputation was something Henry cared very little about.

He slept soundly until his alarm-clock woke him.

9

THREE weeks proved altogether too long a period to stay away from Eden.

Henry fretted impatiently through the first week and part of another, but by the time Friday of the second week arrived he had made up his mind to end his self-imposed exile. He would spend the whole of the coming week-end pottering openly around Eden, defying all comers to oppose his claim.

It was mid-morning on Saturday before he plucked up the courage to go. Summer had arrived in all its splendour and he was dressed incongruously in shorts, open-necked shirt and wellington boots. But once again his mood was at odds with the weather.

Crouched behind the wheel of his Rover and hooding his eyes against the sun he felt like a condemned man, with no appetite, facing a last, unwanted, hearty breakfast. His feeling of foreboding was so strong that he almost turned back, abandoning the ill-fated experiment, writing it off as a wild and unattainable dream. The voice of conscience assured him repeatedly that his impudent annexing of Eden could not have gone unnoticed. Someone would be lying in wait there, full of righteous indignation and a thirst for retribution, backed up by a Platoon of Militia or the local constable at least.

Thinking of policemen, he was reminded of the incident of the stranded launch. That was one point in his favour, but it would give him no indemnity from police action. In fact, the small issue might hasten Henry's downfall by concentrating interest on him. Constable Crossley had seemed a reasonable fellow, but he had his job to do and must be expected to have done it.

By this time, High Court Writs

would have been sworn out and all the majesty of a violated Law would be massed to await the arrival of the upstart Henry Crumblestone. Agents of Authority would have spent the past fortnight preparing their case against the owner of that none too common name and the Bum-bailiffs would be there in force, eager to bear him into custody.

In the event, Henry's fears proved groundless.

Even before climbing from his car he could see that his fence was still in place. That handsome painted notice, like a frozen banner, remained proudly erect, its legend unimpaired.

Henry felt his nerves creak and slacken as he took a long, possessive look at Eden. It was a tangled and jungly place, but he loved it. And happily, nothing had changed. The massive chain-link fence still flanked the Marina to his left and the solid bridge — eternal — stretched away to his right. The reed clumps still waved their olive tops. The slow-moving waters of the Wissey still poured out under the bridge span and rolled onwards to the distant sea.

For the first time since the scheme's inception, Henry began to experience a true feeling of ownership — began to believe that his shining dream could become wonderful reality. Nobody resented his intrusion. It was really going to work.

The time had come for the next symbolic step.

Fumbling in the pocket of his shorts he took out the shiny key, removed the padlock and flung back the small gate. Then, with the air of a dignitary performing an opening ceremony, he advanced.

One step — two steps — three steps.

Henry was now completely surrounded by his own land, a Monarch, squarely installed in his own kingdom.

★ ★ ★

On that first momentous Saturday he did little more than extend his original survey, beginning from The Fortress and moving slowly outward, fanwise, treading paths and marking ditches. He grubbed out a few clumps of isolated rushes and pruned the worst of the overhanging shrubs in a small area. Even so, when the day was over he felt he had established beyond doubt the value of Eden as a holding.

He was back again, bright and early on the following day, armed with an assortment of tools, to begin the task of transforming Eden into a garden worthy of the name. He had barely set his sickle against the first fringes of reeds when a familiar voice assailed his ears.

"Hoy!" it said.

Henry straightened up and looked towards the river. A motor launch was drifting slowly downstream a few feet clear of the bank. It was small and brightly painted and its engine was silent. There were two men in the launch and Henry recognised them both.

Standing splay-legged at the helm was the large, ill-tempered man from the Wiscliffe Marina, Basil Jenks. He was splendidly arrayed in an all white outfit of trousers, open-necked shirt and soft-peaked cap. His whole rig looked clean and newly pressed and was in sharp contrast with his face, which was the usual beefy red.

His companion was propped, unmoving, against the stern. He was a wizened runt of a man, bald-headed and with weaselly features, more sombrely dressed in dark trousers and a red roll-neck sweater. In the instant of recognition, Henry had him classified as 'the accomplice'. He was exactly the type who would cut a man's moorings and set his punt adrift.

Frank Finch!

Henry had known him since boyhood and had disliked him then for his unruly habits, his bitter nature and his persistent bullying. He had heard nothing since to convince him that Finch was in any way reformed.

Finch was a Property Repairer of doubtful quality, whose back-street business had blossomed remarkably since his election as a District Councillor for one of the Wiscliffe wards. He had the dried-up, wrinkled appearance of a puppet — and if the weight of local rumour meant anything at all he was precisely that — a puppet manipulated by the other more flamboyant occupant of the launch.

Basil Jenks looked no more pleased than at their last meeting. He was looking angrily at Henry, who had no doubt that it was Jenks who had spoken. As if to confirm the fact and underline his displeasure, Jenks said again, arrogantly:-

"Hoy!"

Henry felt the flood of animosity conveyed by the single word, but he was in no mood to put up with more intimidation by this loud-mouthed bully.

"Are you addressing me?" he enquired, haughtily.

"I should have thought that was obvious," Jenks sneered. "What do you think you're doing there?"

Henry's heart sank towards his wellingtons.

The words were a direct challenge to his occupancy and could only herald another ordering off. He had always intended to leave as gracefully as possible the moment some rightful owner showed up to question his presence and he had expected the moment to be painful. But it would be doubly painful to be ousted by the tyrant Jenks, who seemed to have a flair for making people feel small.

And yet, Jenks was a known blusterer. He was blustering now, and bluster alone was no evidence of proprietary rights. To hell and back with Jenks! A seed of rebellion germinating at lightning speed, caused Henry to stand his ground.

"Minding my own business," he

retorted. "And I suggest you do the same."

By this time the launch had drifted close inshore and to stay its passage, Jenks grasped a handful of bankside vegetation and held on.

"Who told you you could hack those reeds about?" he enquired belligerently.

Who indeed? Henry was all too well aware that every time he snipped off a reed-head he violated somebody else's rights. But who could that somebody be? Not the Wiscliffe Yachting Marina and Caravan Club if he had read the signs aright, else why had they excluded the land in such an obvious way with their expensive fence. And with a thrill of intuition, he realised it could not be Jenks, either. Jenks would not have dallied off-shore if he claimed the land — he would have invaded. Henry decided to persist with his bold face.

"I can do what I want with my own land."

"Your land?" Jenks queried, gaping.

"That's right. My land. I bought it."

The lie grated on Henry's tongue, but he was glad he'd voiced it. The big man's face turned a brighter crimson, but at least he said nothing, when he might have ranted and cursed and mouthed threats. He might have been outraged, but he was merely annoyed. Henry watched Jenks closely as he scowled and puzzled over the news. He was going to accept it. He *really was* going to accept it.

"See that fence?" Jenks said finally, nodding his massive head towards the structure. "That's our fence, Crumblestone, and t'other side of it is our property. Keep off that fence if you know what's good for you. If I find the slightest damage done to that fence — even a scratch — I'll have the law down on you like a ton of bricks."

The words were a surrender and Henry saw a chance to assert his victory. Turning aside from Jenks, he pointed dramatically back in the direction of the road.

"You see that notice-board, Jenks?" he thundered. "I put it there — and if you take the trouble to read it you'll find that I have possessions as well as you and your tin-pot Marina. 'Trespassers will be prosecuted.' That's what it says Jenks." He turned back and pointed to the hand with which Jenks still grasped the reeds. "And you're trespassing at this very minute. So let go my reeds at once and clear off. Otherwise you'll find my notice means what it says."

"Humph!" Jenks spluttered in anger. But he released his hold and the launch slowly resumed its drift.

"You keep away, Crumblestone. You hear?" He shouted as a parthian shot.

* * *

The engine of the launch fired and the craft leapt forward in response to the whirring screw. Henry watched as Jenks steered into the mouth of the

105

Yachting Marina's channel and passed from his sight.

He was filled with joy and with a sense of new found power. This was not the first time he had publicly acknowledged his claim to the land, but it was the first time he had flexed metaphorical muscles and raised his voice to protect it. There were certain to be other battles, but he had won the first.

Above all men, Basil Jenks had been the likeliest to challenge Henry's occupation.

Jenks had done his best to challenge it.

But he had failed.

10

THE Jenks incident was a fillip to Henry's spirits.

In the course of the next few weeks he worked hard at the shaping of his new acquisition, spending hour after hour and evening after evening, landscaping the little patch of ground. He mapped the complete triangle to his own satisfaction, producing elaborate sketches on which he marked the type and variance of terrain.

Extending downstream from the bridge and parallel with the water's edge there was a fifty yard strip of bank, heavily clothed with rushes and scrub-willow but firmly solid at base. The lower end of this strip degenerated into marsh and there was a crescent of seemingly bottomless bog lying between the firm bank and the upper edge of Lake Ceylon. Quite evidently it was this softness of soil that had caused erosion, leading to the formation of the little pool and its approach channel cutting inwards from the river.

Immediately below Lake Ceylon and reachable only by detour, was the final section of the new fence erected by Basil Jenks and his associates. They had built the fence as a deterrent to Henry himself, and he had been horrified at the time. Now, in retrospect, he was delighted that they had done so. By effectively marking the limits of the Marina's territory, Jenks had paved the way for Henry's claim. He could not have realised the unintentional benevolence in his own pointedly hostile act.

Moving inland from the river's edge, Henry was confronted by a curious mosaic of land textures. Centrally in the triangle there was a large patch of firm ground covered with rank grass and clumps of rushes. Henry estimated it to be the size of half a tennis-court. Marshy ground surrounded this patch on three sides, though much of the marsh was shallow enough to be waded in safety and some of it was only inches deep. On the side away from the river and nearest the road, the strip of marsh was no more than a few feet wide at its widest point, and uniformly shallow. The remainder of the triangle as it narrowed toward's Henry's little fence was composed of firm soil, well grassed.

On the opposite side of the central patch — between it and the river bank — the area of marsh was up to ten yards wide and there was soft, stinking mud towards its centre. That part of Eden, if left in its present state, would be unusable, but Henry had not the slightest intention of leaving it in its present state.

Below the central patch on the side bounded by the Marina's fence lay a much larger area of marsh and tussock, stretching as far as the shore of Lake Ceylon. But the soft-going ended there and, running inland from

Lake Ceylon and following the line of the fence, there was an embankment of firmer, stonier ground. This was the strip along which the chain-link fence had been built and it continued almost to Henry's own fence at the apex of the triangle. Half-way along the embankment, on Henry's side, a spring bubbled from the ground and fed its waters into a shallow channel that led thence to the inlet at the neck of Lake Ceylon.

Moving away from there in the direction of Plattsford Bridge, Henry discovered that the fourth (and non-marshy) side of the central plateau was bordered by stunted bushes interwoven with lesser climbing plants. The ground here was firm underfoot and it continued so, right to the stonework of the bridge. It was on this last section that the stone-built Fortress stood.

Once the survey was completed and he had combined his sketches into an overall plan, Henry set to work to enlarge the area of usable land.

He borrowed a scythe — still in good condition in spite of its age — and mastered its use until he could cut broad swathes through the worst of the reeds. He trimmed bushes and trees, hacking out dead wood and removing straggly branches. But some of the bankside willows he left alone, recognising their value as cover both for fish and for angler.

He imported gravel by the ton and bought a wheelbarrow to transfer it from the roadside. It was extremely heavy labour, but he persisted, spreading it in selected places to form a network of paths and to infill some of the smaller hollows and make them solid. He dug and levelled the richer soil to create a pattern of flower beds and by eliminating strips of the shallower marsh he increased the area of the firm central plateau. To augment the plants already growing wild there, he added a variety of his own. Joan, he told himself impishly, would have raised all kinds of a stink if she had realised how many roses and other roots he transplanted from his own garden into the newly formed beds of Eden.

It took Henry two whole evenings to uproot and remove the trunk and branches of a large stricken tree, but his efforts were more than justified by the twin benefits of so doing. Several yards of new and good ground were uncovered beside The Fortress where the tree had lain, and the main trunk and branches — chopped laboriously to length — he used to construct a stable foot-bridge over the worst of the marsh.

Very gradually, the patch of ground was transformed until it became park-like in quality, easy to traverse, dotted with orderly plants, pleasantly contoured, patched with colour, warmly scented and, in its entirety, a delight to behold. On a more practical plane it offered, in addition to the pool, at least a dozen good spots from which Henry could fish the river.

And his activities did not end with

shaping the land.

On warmer days he stripped to bathing trunks, entered the river itself and surveyed the contours and texture of the bed. Wading was impossible immediately below the bridge, where, for ten yards downstream of the first arch, the water depth was a constant ten feet. Henry discovered that fact by rigging a plumb-line from scraps of fishing tackle and treading water as he counted the measure.

Below that stretch there was a short distance of even deeper water, where the river bed plunged to fifteen feet before rising steeply again and levelling off at four feet deep, just upriver of the entrance to Lake Ceylon.

That really deep bit would be a peach of a bream-hole, Henry decided. In summer he'd do better to avoid the deepest parts, but the onset of colder weather would drive the deep-water feeders into that hole. And then he would take his toll.

As for the shallower water, the use

of that suggested itself at once and Henry spent a small fortune on timber. Working neck deep for hours on end, he sank a row of stout posts into the clay of the river bed, linked them with cross-struts and added a level surface of duck-boards to produce a robust and serviceable jetty. Looking later at the finished job, he saw that he had calculated its height nicely. During the highest floods it would be barely covered, whilst at low water it would still afford direct access to a boat.

And boats were very definitely part of the plan.

Initially, he contented himself with the purchase of a small fibre-glass dinghy, but he was determined to increase his fleet to include at least one custom-built fishing punt as soon as funds would allow.

Money was becoming a problem, he discovered.

The expense of development was making severe inroads into his available capital and he experienced the odd qualm when he reminded himself that all this painstaking work would be worthless if the project turned sour. The true owner of the land might still appear. If he did, he would hardly be likely to offer any recompense — and there was no way in which Henry could legally reclaim.

But he had appreciated that risk from the beginning and would not allow it to stay his hand. He continued to labour and to spend. He visited Eden daily and lived and breathed its blossoming. The moment one improvement-task was ended, several more presented themselves, and Henry tackled all of them with boundless enthusiasm.

And also — during this period — he met Sam Little.

★ ★ ★

Their meeting was planned on Sam's part, but it caught Henry completely unawares.

It was a fine, dry evening when

Henry arrived at Eden, parked at the entrance and stepped out along the main pathway which skirted the central plateau and led to the door of The Fortress. He seemed to be entirely alone in Eden, as usual.

Henry had taken to leaving some of his bulkier tools in the old building rather than tote them back and forth in his car. As yet, he had made no attempt to repair The Fortress but in due course he planned to cover the windows and replace some of the roof spars and tiles.

As he approached the front of The Fortress its ricketty door swung open and a man emerged.

He was a complete stranger to Henry, an elderly man, well into his sixties, Henry guessed, and he moved unsteadily with the aid of a walking stick. He was unusually tall, topping Henry's modest five feet seven inches by at least a foot, and whilst his body-bulk was that of a well-proportioned man his height made him look so slim as to seem emaciated. His feet were cased in heavy brown boots, and the legs of a pair of brown cord trousers showed under a too long overcoat which was faded to approximately the same colour. His thick grey hair sprouted like a cabbage over head and ears and his long face was dark and weatherbeaten.

Henry's first thought was that he had disturbed a thief, but the old man had not the manner of a thief. There was nothing furtive about the way he hobbled in Henry's direction, his eyes on Henry's face at every step. Nor was he a tramp. His clothes were faded but not by any means ragged.

The third possibility was a worrying one and Henry convinced himself that it was the true answer. The old man was there to question Henry's occupation of the land.

Well, the confrontation might be undesired, but it was certainly not unexpected, and Henry firmed his will as he advanced to meet the man and hear his challenge.

"You must be Mr Crumblestone?" The man said mildly.

"I'm Henry Crumblestone, yes."

"I thought it must be you. I saw your name on the board there." He advanced and held out a massive hand. "Pleased to meet you. My name's Little. Sam Little."

He dropped the walking stick and in an exaggerated gesture, placed the flat of his hand on top of his head, where it looked for all the world like the pointer of a measuring stick. Then, in case his audience might have missed the point, he rolled his eyes upwards to peer at the hand. That done, he threw his head hard back, opened his mouth wide and gargled and shook with mirth.

"Damned silly name for a chap like me, isn't it?" he offered when his laughter had subsided. "Not my fault at all, really. My dad was Fred Little and he only stood five-foot eight. But he married my mother — and she was a big 'un. Between 'em they managed to throw a pup like neither of 'em expected." He paused and peered narrowly down at Henry, as though gauging his reaction. Then he continued:- "So now I can shrink a bit, or change my name, or just put up with it. And that's what I've always done, Mr Crumblestone. Put up with it, I mean."

He laughed loudly again in the same curious manner and his mood was so infectious that Henry was moved to join in. At the end of the second bout of laughter, all Henry's fears had disappeared and he was involved in a brand new friendship.

Sam Little was a widower without children. He had spent a lifetime in farming, latterly as a manager, and had retired four years earlier. Now he lived alone in a small terraced cottage a short half-mile away on the Plattsford Road and he liked to go walking in nice weather.

"I saw all the work you'd done here," he explained. "You've made a right good job of it, Mr Crumblestone.

I've stood up yonder on the bridge and looked it over, but I wanted to feel it under my feet. I didn't think you'd mind if I had a little walk round, so here I am. You don't mind, do you?" he finished, tilting his head to one side and squinting down at Henry.

"Not the least bit, Mr Little," Henry assured him with a wide grin. "I'd be glad to see you here any time. Just make the place your own."

It occurred to Henry about then, that he had never been able to refuse that kind of request and — even if he had disliked the man and resented his intrusion — he would still have felt compelled to issue the invitation.

Thankfully, none of that applied to Sam Little. Right from their first meeting Henry had had the strong feeling that there was affinity between himself and the old man.

He wanted Sam to be there.

11

AND Sam Little wanted to be there also.

That much was plain to see. From the date of their first meeting, Sam appeared regularly, once or twice a week, tapping his stick across the bridge and strolling into Eden with the air of a holidaymaker at the seaside. He loved to spend an hour or two in Henry's company, watching the younger man as he tended his plants and tinkered with his equipment. Sam's brand of conversation was always lively and interesting and he was a rich source of anecdote about the district and its people.

He even became a convert to the gentle art of angling, perching himself on the river bank at Henry's side and enthusing over every wriggling fish that came ashore. He was unsparing with both criticism and praise, applauding Henry for his successes and greeting his failures with excited and scathing censure. Supplied with a rod of his own, he made a determined effort to emulate Henry and before long he was able to hook and land fish more or less unaided.

"I've lived by this river all my life," he chortled, when things were going well and he was in danger of becoming an addict. "And I've seen thousands of crazy buggers at this worm-drowning lark. But there's something in it, Henry, I've got to give you that. Even the little 'uns tug about a bit."

Henry could see one of his best rods in deadly danger.

"Watch your rod-tip, man!" he shouted. "You missed that willow by half an inch. Now, swing it further out towards . . . no . . . further than that, damn you! Here, Sam. Give it to me, for God's sake!"

"It's these pins of mine," Sam Little explained, when Henry cajoled him to visit Eden more often. "I can't get about like I used to. It's the rheumatics."

"That's no excuse, Sam. I've got a car yonder. I can pick you up and drop you here inside five minutes."

But Sam had an old countryman's aversion to modern machines and was particularly caustic about motor cars.

"Don't you bring that old bloody smoke-box anywhere near my house," he insisted. "Dirty smelly things they are. I'd have 'em banned."

In these and like ways, the two men fell-out with each other constantly, without ever sounding an aggressive note. It was the stuff that knits men together and it made them firm friends.

When Henry decided to carry out much needed repairs to The Fortress, Sam superintended the job and tongue-lashed the perspiring worker if he faltered in his efforts or if his work failed to achieve Sam's exacting standards. And Henry, who since his schooldays had taken orders from no man, bent his shoulders to the crack of Sam's whip and revelled in the experience.

The heavy stone tiles were removed from the roof and stacked for re-use. Henry bought new timbers and fitted them in place with bolts and brackets. At the start of the operation he had no knowledge of the art of tiling, but before the roof was finished he had half decided — whimsically — to throw up his well paid job and become a builder.

He purchased a job-lot of glass and window-frames and glazed the fortress throughout, renewed the door and fitted a new lock to which he and Sam Little held a key, repaired the stonework and patched weak places with improvised mortar, dug and levelled the floor, installed a coke-stove and flue and wheelbarrowed in a supply of fuel against the onset of winter.

Between them they made The Fortress habitable by moving in a scratching of furniture, old chairs and tables donated by Sam and mats and curtains which

Henry acquired cheaply from sale-rooms and market stalls. Under their ministrations the old stone building became a comfortable den, affording shelter in wet weather and a place to loll and chat whenever the mood beset them.

★ ★ ★

Ironically, it was Sam Little the welcome companion, who first brought Henry disturbing news. The occasion found Sam in sombre humour and when Henry chaffed him about it he delivered the tidings with visible reluctance.

"You'll lose this place, eventually, Henry. You'll be tossed out. I suppose you know that?"

Henry's reaction was cautious. He'd wondered for some time whether he ought to confide in Sam, whether he should explain his own precarious position at Eden. But the old man always seemed so blissfully content to share the place as it was, that it seemed a shame to burden him with knowledge of Henry's insecurity. Now though, there was a hint in Sam's words that he might have found out the truth.

"Lose Eden?" Henry prevaricated. "How come?"

"You know there's a new bridge coming through?"

"A new bridge?" Henry echoed stupidly, his thoughts flying in a new direction. "Where did you hear that tale?"

"Oh it's no tale." Sam said seriously. "The County Council have had it on their books for a while. I remember one or two folk writing to the papers about it. But that was a few years back, and I'd forgotten all about it till last night, when one chap told me they'll be announcing it soon."

Impossible not to be shocked and puzzled by the news.

"Funny I've never heard about it," Henry said. "Anyway, what do we want with a new bridge, Sam? What's amiss with the one we've got?"

"Nothing! They're not proposing to knock it down. The new one isn't *instead of*, it's *as well as*."

"Two bridges?"

"So I'm told. It's all these poisonous bloody cars that come piling through. You know yourself, Henry, there's all sorts of snarl-ups here in summer, when half the folk in Christendom want to drive from Plattsford to Wiscliffe and back again. They're hoping to stop that. The idea is to make the old bridge one-way — for traffic coming in to Wiscliffe — and chuck another bridge over, to take the traffic moving out."

"And they're going to build it here?"

"Slap bang here, Henry, as I understand it. Straight across Eden. There'll be dual-carriageway then, across the Wissey and for a few hundred yards on each side."

Henry allowed his eyes to wander over the neat half-acre and he was filled with overwhelming sadness.

"It isn't fair, Sam," he groaned.

"Not after all the work we've done here. They can't just rip it all up."

"It's a credit to you, that's for sure," Sam said. "But they *can* rip it up, Henry, and that's what they *will* do."

"So you're telling me I've got to go. Is that it?"

"Looks like it." Sam was equally doleful. "I wouldn't think of moving just yet though. It's always a slow job with the County. I should think it'll be at least a couple of years before they even get started."

A couple of years!

Well, at least that was something. Henry's spirits rose a notch or two as he considered the point. There was much to enjoy in Eden and it would be a sad day when he had to leave, but if he could stay for as long as two years, that would be twenty times the term of occupancy he had originally hoped for. Sam noticed the improvement in Henry's mood and his eyes twinkled.

"There'll have to be a Public Enquiry," he pointed out, "and they'll listen to objections. So why don't you object, Henry? I'd be happy to go along and support you."

"I can't object."

"Can't? I don't understand you. Do you mean 'won't'?"

Once again, Henry considered explaining his position to Sam, but for the same reasons as before, he rejected the notion.

"Can't or won't," he said huffily. "There'll be no objection from me."

"Then we'll have to make the most of Eden while we've still got the chance," Sam Little said.

"That we will, Sam," Henry agreed.

★ ★ ★

And in the enjoyment and enterprise of succeeding days, Henry pushed the matter of the coming new bridge into the back of his mind. He continued to spend all his spare time at Eden, and every hour of it was filled with great reward.

Henry's biggest disappointment — perhaps his only true disappointment — was the effect his industry had on Lake Ceylon.

He had cut down some of the profuse growth surrounding the pool and could now reach its waters comfortably with a well-aimed cast from upstream. But whenever he did so, his efforts were wasted. He spent a number of warm evenings fishing there — flicking morsel after tempting morsel of varied baits into the slow-moving water — but there was never a take, or even an offer.

And one particularly hot afternoon, when the sun was hot and high and the Wissey half a foot below its normal level, he discovered why.

The shoal of chub, it seemed, no longer occupied the pool. By standing on tip-toe at the nearest point of approach he could see straight into the depths of Lake Ceylon, could run his eyes over every inch of the eroded bottom beneath the trickling inlet spring.

The pool was quite empty.

Not a bleak or a minnow swam there. Something had driven them away, and when he thought about it, Henry himself was the most probable cause. His presence must have scared them. His reed-clearing, his work in building the jetty and the splashing and general disturbance his boats caused, all must have combined to convince the chub that there were more peaceful places to be found elsewhere.

As a breed, chub thrived in abundant natural cover. Henry knew all about that, yet thoughtlessly he now realised, he had removed too much of it.

It was an unhappy discovery, but Henry cheered himself with the thought that in destroying one good swim he had been able to create so many others. None of the others would ever be quite so magic as Lake Ceylon, but they would all be productive in their turn. And all of them — in a possessory sense at least — were entirely his own.

Just as he was turning away from the small pool, Henry picked up a sluggish movement from the corner of his eye. It was right at the pool's outer edge, where the slow sweep of the main river formed a line of turbulence across the entrance. He strained his eyes until he could make out the origin of the movement.

It was an eel — and an unusually large specimen.

Henry watched it as it swam sinuously into full view, traversed the length of Lake Ceylon and came to rest with its body corrugated on the grey bottom, its probing nose waving in the incoming trickle.

Henry disliked eels on principle.

He had hooked and landed many of the great long slimy creatures over the years, but he had never enjoyed the process. They fouled his clothes with slime, gorged his hooks down to their tails and — if not handled carefully — were capable of reducing yards of good nylon line to a greasy, unsalvageable tangle.

But eels were natural denizens of the Wissey, as they were of any other river, and he was not particularly dismayed by the presence of a giant of the species.

After all, he told himself comfortably, *there was the best of precedent for a serpent in Eden.*

12

AS Henry Crumblestone was soon to learn, a serpent was about to enter Eden, bringing evil to the little plot, but it was not the stately and harmless eel.

And until the evil became manifest, Henry's project seemed to prosper. His moral victory over Basil Jenks had set the seal on Henry's success and in its wake he felt more firmly established than ever before. His nightly visits to the peaceful garden became a pilgrimage of almost holy quality.

By late summer, the bulk of the heavy work was done, and he coped easily with the few running tasks of weeding his plants, maintaining paths, repairing the minor ravages of flood and weather and generally keeping the place in order. These things apart, he found he could spend most of his time fishing, paddling his boats or merely pottering about and keeping a proprietary eye on his possessions.

With Sam Little's help, he had made a host of improvements and additions. There were three foot-bridges now, linking the pattern of paths and making virtually the whole of Eden accessible. They had constructed a wooden bench overlooking the jetty and on fine evenings the pair of them would sit chatting and making plans as they watched the smooth drifting waters of the Wissey. A tidy man by nature, Henry had installed litter-bins at strategic points and in a cleared space behind The Fortress he built a compost box and an incinerator for disposing of collected rubbish. He assembled a store of tools and equipment in a corner of The Fortress's single room and a pile of usable timber and building materials outside the building.

The white fibre-glass dinghy bobbing at the jetty had been joined by a first class punt, complete with built-in live-bait well. It was a second-hand job, but had been maintained in good condition and it cost Henry rather more than he wanted to pay. But it looked handsome at the jetty and would pay for itself in use within a couple of years.

A couple of years!

But he might have at least that long. Certainly nothing more had been said locally about the new bridge. He would act as though it might never happen, Henry decided as he laboured by the river, excavating a gentle sloping channel alongside the jetty, to serve as a ramp for beaching or launching the boats.

Sam contributed a variety of small items to the common fund, but the one that pleased Henry most was a pressure-lamp, in mint condition, which he had found amongst forgotten bric-a-brac at home. They installed the lamp in The Fortress and laid in a supply of fuel and spare burners, so that as the evenings drew in they could stay on for an hour after dark, working or talking in the lighted room.

Thus, their time in Eden was spent in an atmosphere of comfort and seemingly endless peace. And when that peace was shattered it happened by degrees — almost imperceptibly.

The first indication came when Henry arrived one evening to find his notice-board and post missing. At first he feared it had been stolen, but in fact it had only been uprooted and flung amongst the long grass beside the footstones of the bridge. He found it after a search, and to his relief it was quite undamaged. So he enlarged the post-hole in the ground, re-erected the notice-board and tamped the earth firmly down around it, grumbling the while about the youth of today and their inability to pass anything of value without seeking to destroy it.

But it was a small annoyance.

That kind of thing was liable to happen occasionally in the best of areas. Vandals had found their way to Eden and indulged in their petty little pranks. Whoever they were he felt reasonably confident they would not return. So he closed his mind to the incident, and when darkness came he drove home in his usual happy mood.

The very next evening when he drew up beside the entrance he noticed at once that the notice-board was missing again. This time it had been torn from the post, which was still standing. For once, Sam Little had reached Eden ahead of him and Henry found Sam in The Fortress, working on the notice-board with a paraffin-soaked rag. The face of the notice — all Henry's beautifully printed words — had been daubed with black paint.

"I can get most of it off all right," Sam said philosophically. "Though how much good this has done anybody I can't see for the life of me. It's just destruction for its own sake. Still, not to worry, Henry. The buggers won't come twice."

"That's the mistake I made yesterday,"

Henry said ruefully, and he explained that this was the second visitation.

"The buggers want catching then," Sam vowed. "I'd have a word with the bobbies if I were you. If they just sent a car up here for a night or two — that would stop it."

Sam's was the obvious solution, of course, and for a while Henry considered the advice. Was there no end to the aimless destructiveness that had become so rampant lately? It was hard to have any kind of sympathy with the developing generation of louts and wreckers. Nasty selfish yobboes they were, who had long been a source of trouble and disruption in the towns and villages of the area.

And yet, Eden was miles away from even the nearest village. Henry would not have expected to be much bothered in this remote spot. But the evidence was there. He *was* being bothered. Society seemed powerless these days to control the growing army of layabouts who showed so little respect for other people's property — who committed their outrages with such impunity.

It really was time something was done about it. This sort of thing could not be allowed to go on. Henry made a mental note to call at the Police Station as soon as he got back to Wiscliffe and complain in the strongest possible terms about this wanton damage to his property.

And then — using the same mental pen — he erased the note.

Because the truth was borne on Henry Crumblestone that he had no firm foundation on which to base such a complaint. He had annexed Eden without encountering the slightest objection so far, but he could not claim to truly own it. He had none of the legal rights of an owner, however much he chose to lie.

He'd kept his nerve when telling the lie to Jenks of the Marina, but he would have no stomach for falsehood when talking to the police. Those men had spent a lifetime dealing with liars and could quell the false tongue with a look. It was a fact that he'd faced up to Constable Crossley without any difficulty, but then the boot had been squarely on the other foot. Crossley had come seeking favours, with his mind full of boats and boating. Henry's role had been that of benefactor and Constable Crossley would have found it all too easy to view him in that light.

The Police, though, were something else again. He would have to consider them as distinct from a single friendly policeman. In Henry's mind *the police* loomed large as a powerful, versatile and intellectual agency, well versed in grappling with the deeper problems of law. *The police* were much less likely than Constable Crossley alone — or than Basil Jenks alone, for that matter — to accept his claim on face value.

In particular, *the police* would not be easy to hoodwink on the vital question of ownership of land. They would have detailed maps of the area, cataloguing every plot and acre and listing the persons to whom the various parcels belonged. Therefore, Henry could not safely seek their aid against vandals, thieves or malcontents of any kind.

Henry was vulnerable.

If he maintained a discreet silence there was a chance that the police might remain in ignorance of his act of squatting, but if he were foolish enough to lead them to Eden on the heels of a trivial complaint, they'd realise the truth for certain-sure. Besides, the spot of trouble Henry was having could only be a passing phase. Flying in the teeth of the old adage, lightning had struck twice in exactly the same place, but coincidence could have no longer arm than that. A third bolt was out of the question.

Impossible, though, to explain all this to Sam. Henry had been right to keep Sam in the dark — and these visitations made no difference to the basic rightness of his case. So he shrugged Sam's advice aside.

"It isn't worth the trouble," he

averred. "The police have their work cut out to deal with serious crime. It wouldn't be right to go chasing off to them over every bit of nuisance. No — we can manage without the police, Sam. We'll just be a bit more vigilant, that's all."

"All right then, Henry. You can leave it to me." Sam Little said firmly. "I'll be bobbing up here a lot more often from now on. I'll bring a bit of lunch and camp out in The Fortress — and pity help the buggers if I catch 'em."

"I'd rather you kept away," Henry said anxiously.

"Oh! Like that is it? That's not the way you've been talking up to now. But it's quite all right, Henry. If you're sick of me. If you want me to stop coming . . . "

The hurt look on Sam Little's face — completely spurious though it was — made Henry burst out laughing, and very soon both men were in better humour.

"But I don't want you here, Sam,"

Henry repeated. "Not when I'm away. We can do without heroics. If we're ever going to lick this problem we'll do it together."

* * *

Henry's notice-board was not completely ruined.

Sam worked hard with his rag, soaking off the gouts of paint while striving to keep the painted words legible. After an hour's careful rubbing there was a marked improvement and Henry was satisfied with the finished job.

A lot of the surface varnish had been rubbed away, and a new coat was indicated, but that was something he would have to leave for another time. He refixed the notice to its post, using six-inch nails which he clenched on the reverse side, and it seemed almost as good as new.

But both men were still bitterly annoyed about the damage and ready to take any necessary steps to avoid a repetition.

"Tomorrow's Saturday," Sam pointed out. "What time do you figure on coming here?"

"Crack of dawn without a doubt," Henry said. "I'm going to spend all Saturday and all Sunday here, from dawn till dark. As long as I'm here, there'll be no trouble."

"As long as *we're* here, Henry," Sam corrected, "because you've got a full-time partner this week-end."

13

IT rained hard on Saturday morning. There was a spell of weak sunshine in the afternoon, but before the eaves of The Fortress had ceased to drip the rain clouds returned and resumed their weeping.

Sunday morning was fine, but before mid-day the clouds gathered and a soaking drizzle began to fall. It continued to drizzle throughout the afternoon.

Henry and Sam spent most of their two days huddled in The Fortress. The unexpected chilly spell had caught them unawares. Henry wanted to light the coke-stove, to 'give it a trial run' as he put it, but Sam argued that it was pointless to run the thing for an odd hour, and his view prevailed.

So they chatted and brooded and peered out on Eden through gloomy windows. Waiting in those conditions was tedious but neither would admit it. Where one alone might have weakened, both contained their boredom and were strong.

As a trap, their vigil was a waste of time.

Apart from a steady stream of traffic passing along the Plattsford/Wiscliffe Road and a few bedraggled oarsmen using the river, they saw no movement in the vicinity of Eden.

But as a deterrent it seemed to have been effective.

Certainly, when they inspected the plot all over as darkness approached on the second day, there was no sign of damage. Gratified, they spent some time discussing why this should be. As Sam pointed out, they had mostly kept out of sight, so any would-be intruders would not have known they were there. Not so, Henry argued, pointing out that his Rover had spent both days parked at the roadside adjacent to Eden. The car alone would have been enough to keep people away.

There was no positive answer to the question. Maybe the atrocious weather had been sufficient of itself to fend off trouble-makers? Or again, maybe the true reason was the happiest possible reason — that the vandals had had their fun and grown tired of attacking Eden.

They convinced themselves that the last reason was the likeliest. When they parted that night, it was to the echo of a shared view that Eden would suffer no more.

* * *

On the following evening, Henry came to Eden in the best of moods.

He had prepared a batch of flour-paste in several unusual flavours and aimed to see if the fat roach that lived in the Wissey would find it palatable. He had his eye on a fine looking spot close to the first arch of Plattsford Bridge, where the water ran dark and deep and there was a good trotting

148

current just off the trailing branch-tips of a willow. He had never tried that particular peg before, but he had high hopes of it.

There was to be no fishing that evening.

Climbing from his car, Henry noticed with a feeling of dismay that there was now a broad gateway into Eden. His fence had been removed entirely. He stepped warily onto the plot and the first thing to catch his eye was a spiral of smoke curling upwards in the vicinity of The Fortress.

When he reached it, the fire was almost out. His wood stack had suffered very little and the only damage was a few lengths of timber charred and blackened, but his fence had turned to nothing in the flames. Charred scraps of timber, smoking hot wire and a twisted padlock were all that remained.

Why not his notice-board for God's sake? In his anger, Henry was conscious of a brief masochistic wish to have yet more hurt visited on him. Turning, he confirmed that the notice-board was still in place. It surprised him that they had not added it to the bonfire. Because these were the same vandals, he felt absolutely sure of that, and they'd had two goes at the notice-board previously.

So why had they left it this time?

The point probably had no significance.

★ ★ ★

It took Henry several days to obtain new fencing material and during that time the gateway to Eden stood wide open.

On Tuesday, he discovered that somebody had taken advantage of the gap. A pile of unwholesome looking domestic rubbish had been tipped and spread about. Was it the work of some opportunist litter-lout? It was common practice for some people to load up their rubbish and cruise their cars along country lanes, looking for suitable dumping spots.

But Henry didn't think so.

Faint in the soil he could see the marks of tyred wheels. They were motor tyres all right, but not wide enough apart to be fitted to a motor car. Some type of two-wheeled barrow or hand-cart had probably made the marks.

But the damage this time could be easily remedied if the unpleasant smell could be borne. Henry unlocked The Fortress intending to get out a brush, shovel and wheelbarrow to cart the unsightly mess to his incinerator and dispose of it. But before collecting the tools, he walked round to look at the incinerator.

It was missing.

The rough brick base remained, but the perforated forty-gallon oil-drum, so efficient as a furnace, was missing. There was clear indication of what had happened to the drum. It had been tilted on edge and rolled away, and the clean cut marks of its progress could be seen in the soil. Henry followed the marks until they ended at the very brink of the river — and the story was complete.

Tossed into deep water the drum would sink within seconds and on reaching the bed of the river it would trundle along till it settled in a deep hole. After that, it would lie, gathering silt, perhaps for ever.

In terms of value, the item was no great loss. Oil-drums like it could be picked up cheaply enough, and half an hour with a hammer and cold chisel would convert a fresh drum to the condition of its predecessor. But as a symptom of a disease the loss of the incinerator was significant. It killed any hope that the attacks of vandalism might have ceased.

On his way back from the river, Henry could plainly see the widespread stain of filth that contaminated Eden and he ached to be rid of it. One possible method was to shovel it into his litter bins as a temporary measure until he could replace the incinerator. If he collected the bins together and shovelled the rubbish into them . . .

He looked around. All his litter bins were missing.

They had been metal containers too. They would have been pitched into the river, he felt sure. Like the incinerator, they would cost very little to replace.

But in terms of nuisance value the whole business was starting to cost Henry dear. These were not outbreaks of casual vandalism, not devil's work found for idle hands. There was something horribly pointed and personal about the systematic destruction of his possessions.

In desperation, Henry gathered the rubbish together in a pile and set fire to it. There would be some residual damage to an area of grass, but that was preferable to living with a malodorous heap of muck. The burning was an almost complete success. When darkness came, nothing remained but a pile of embers and they had almost ceased to glow. On Wednesday evening the postscript had been added. His notice-board had once again been uprooted.

He found it easily, but there was no question this time of cleaning it up. Someone had re-kindled the remains of Henry's fire and burned the notice-board to ashes. A few of the hand-painted letters could still be seen, outlined in powdery white, but at a touch they crumbled to dust.

Advancing, he entered a scene of ruin. A shambles.

A pick-axe or some similar tool had been used to hack pits and channels in his gravel paths. Flowers and shrubs had been uprooted and thrown aside to die. His carefully tended garden beds had been gouged apart and freshly dug soil was scattered everywhere.

Henry was not demonstrative or emotional by nature, but seeing the senseless destruction he felt on the verge of tears. There was no urge in him to repair or replace, and he would have left the mess and gone home if Sam Little had not come tapping onto the bridge at that moment.

Sam was bitterly upset too, but practical.

He helped Henry to collect the scattered soil, replant shrubs and fill and flatten the scars in the paths. All evening he aimed wasted curses and threats at the unseen enemy and he was firmly minded to move his bed to The Fortress and live there until the attacks ended.

Sam's attitude was good for Henry, if his scheme was not. In the course of talking Sam out of it — and that was no easy task — he talked himself into a more philosophical mood and could face the outbreaks of vandalism in better heart.

Which was just as well in the circumstances.

On Thursday evening, Henry was surprised to see what seemed to be dead trees sprouting from the reed-bed over towards the river. On closer inspection he found that his main foot-bridge had been torn up and some of the components were missing. Fearing worse, he checked everything. Nothing else appeared to have been damaged, but the fact did little to appease him.

Angrily, he set to work to repair the bridge and by the onset of dark it was usable again.

But it would never be as stable as it had been before.

★ ★ ★

It was later than usual when Henry reached Eden on the Friday evening because he had spent time in Wiscliffe to collect a supply of metal fencing posts and new wire.

Impossible, he knew, to put the fence up forthwith, but tomorrow was Saturday and he would have ample time to do it then. Meanwhile, he proposed to lock the materials in The Fortress, for safety.

But first of all, he looked for damage.

Henry was certain by this time that a nightly attack was quite inevitable. The question had ceased to be *whether* he would find damage — was now an unequivocal *where* and *what*? At first glance he could see nothing, but he was a long way from being persuaded by the hopeful sign.

And his pessimism proved to be justified.

Approaching The Fortress he felt the crackle of breaking glass under his feet and instinctively he looked towards the front window space. It was broken. All four small panes had been smashed to bits.

Henry dropped his burden of metal fencing and cursed aloud in despair, but even as he mouthed blasphemies he became aware of something much more ominous. The door of The Fortress was unlocked and slightly ajar.

Not forced open — *unlocked* — and the key was still in the lock with a dozen other keys and a black leather thong hanging in a bunch below it.

Sam's keys! He recognised them at once.

Henry rushed to the door and pushed to open it. The door remained stubbornly ajar, held in that position by some obstruction inside. He could neither see what hindered nor pass through the gap — and a premonition warned him not to attempt to force the door open.

He ran round to the side facing the river. That window was broken too — completely — frame and smashed glass ripped out of the cavity. He leapt to the sill, paused momentarily, then heaved himself inside.

The first thing to impress itself on his senses was a strong smell of paraffin and automatically his eyes went to the corner where fuel for the lamp had been stored. The paraffin can was upended, a broad, damp patch on the ground being the only remains of its contents.

But the grey bundle lying close

against the door had Henry's most earnest attention, and even in the half-light recognition was instant.

Sam Little! The bastards had killed him!

★ ★ ★

Sam was unconscious, not dead, but he had taken a cruel blow.

A long cut divided the flesh of his left cheek and the edges of the gash still oozed blood. There was blood on his face, on his neck and on the side of his head. A quantity of blood had soaked into his shirt and formed a large sticky patch across collar and shoulders.

His heavy body lay supine, completely blocking the door, and flecks of blood were visible on his profuse grey hair.

Henry dropped to his knees, took hold of the old man's shoulders and lifted gently. As he did so, Sam's eyes flickered and he groaned. The gruff sound and the tiny spasm of movement filled Henry with overwhelming relief.

Sam opened his eyes and grinned weakly.

"You're miles too late again, old mate," he said.

14

THE Waiting-room in the Casualty Department at Wiscliffe General Hospital was a gloomy and draughty place, filled with rows of uncomfortable plastic chairs, many of them occupied by dejected-looking patients, and the whole imbued with a composite odour of sweat, lint and disinfectant. But, sitting on the front row alongside Sam Little, Henry Crumblestone was barely conscious of the scene around him.

Henry was a very angry man.

Angry in the main because he blamed himself for Sam's injury. There had been more than enough warning of trouble in Eden, but instead of tackling the cause he had been content to bow his head and take the buffets of fate. His reasons had been sound enough, but they were only good reasons so long as the risks were his own risks. It was totally unforgivable that he should have exposed the old man to danger.

If he had taken proper measures early enough, the attack on Sam would never have happened. Proper measures, of course, meant calling the police, and long before now he should have done precisely that. By not doing so, he had shown himself up as an abject coward, even though there were connected repercussions that he had sought to avoid. He had been selfish in the extreme, and as a result poor Sam would probably be scarred for the rest of his life.

It was too late now to undo that particular damage, but at least Henry could make some sort of amends by belatedly doing the right thing. As soon as he had placed Sam and his torn face in the safe hands of a medico, he would head straight for the Police Station and make a clean breast of everything. After that, he would report Sam's injuries and ask for help in tracing

Sam's attackers and bringing them to justice.

"Don't call the police, Henry, whatever you do."

Old Sam had been silent for some time and now Henry was startled by the words springing so aptly to his lips. It was uncanny that he should use those words at this time, almost as though he had divined Henry's thoughts and had deliberately opposed them.

But Henry would not be put off so easily.

"Don't be a fool, Sam," he said roughly. "Smashing up glass and fencing is one thing, but injuring people is something I won't stand for. If they'll do a thing like this there's nothing they won't stoop to. It won't do, Sam. As soon as I'm rid of you, I'm off to report a crime."

Sam gripped his arm and peered at him earnestly.

"You're not to do it Henry. Not on my account. This is a scratch, that's all. I'll not be the cause of trouble for you."

"Trouble? I don't follow you, Sam. When people come and tear my place apart, that's trouble. When somebody takes a shy at you, that's even bigger trouble. But the trouble's happened already. I don't see how going to the police will cause more."

"You know it will. We've been nice and quiet up there so far, but if you call the police they'll come swarming up to Eden, poking about and asking questions. The place won't be peaceful any more."

Henry flashed him a questioning look. This was a complete turn-round on Sam's part and he was puzzled by it.

"I'm not entirely convinced that you're being honest, Sam. Are you sure you've given the right reason?"

But Sam Little was a determined man too.

"You calling me a liar, Henry?" he snapped, his spirit triumphant over pain. "What other bloody reason could there be?"

"What, indeed?

Henry thought the question, but he said nothing.

★ ★ ★

The young Indian Doctor asked questions of Sam, who replied that he had fallen against the edge of a metal door. It was a lame-sounding tale, dreamed up at the last moment, but the Doctor seemed to accept it readily enough.

Sam's injury required a number of stitches and a large padded dressing, but he was not detained. He was discharged into Henry's care, and Henry bore him home in style. Until then, there had been no opportunity for talking at length, but now Sam was anxious to explain.

"I could kick myself," he said hotly. "A bloody child wouldn't have fallen for it. I let you down badly, Henry."

"You let *me* down?" Henry demurred. "I should have thought it was the other way round."

"Nothing of the sort. I should have seen it coming. The signs were all there, Henry. I saw the boat from the bridge, long before I set a foot in Eden. If I'd had as much as half a wit about me, I'd have guessed something was wrong."

"The boat?" Henry said, pricking up his ears. "What boat?"

"I'm coming to that if you'll hang on," Sam said huffily. "There was this little launch tied up at your jetty. It didn't tell me what it should have told me, brainless bugger that I am. I thought it might have been that police chap you mentioned to me, or you'd bought it and hadn't let me know, or you'd got official callers, or some stranger had mistaken the jetty for a public mooring. I thought everything but the obvious thing, that it was something to do with all the bother we've been having."

"Was it Jenks' launch?" Henry said eagerly.

"I don't know."

"Oh come on, Sam. You've seen Jenks passing often enough. You know what his launch looks like. Was his the one you saw?"

"It's no use, Henry. I've told you, I don't know. And I haven't seen Jenks' launch more than a couple of times. With not thinking anything about it, I didn't take much notice. It was sort of light coloured, but I know that doesn't help, because nearly all the launches in these parts are light coloured. Black 'uns are pretty rare."

"Was there anybody aboard?"

"Not that I saw — and I reckon I'd have noticed if there was. There was somebody inside The Fortress though. That's for certain."

"Did you get a good look at him?"

"No, not a bad look either. I didn't get *any* sort of look at him, Henry. I just unlocked the door, stuck my head inside and got a belt round the ear-hole

167

for my trouble. I can't remember a thing that happened after that, till I woke up and you were there."

"But you're sure the door was locked when you got there?"

"Positive. I remember unlocking it."

"And whoever hit you was already inside?"

"Definitely. He had to be."

"Then he'd smashed the windows before you got there, Sam. That's the only way he could have got in. I'm surprised you didn't notice the broken windows when you got there."

"They weren't broken then, Henry. The one at the front wasn't, anyway. I remember looking at the glass on my way to the door. It was all of a piece."

"That's interesting. Did you smell paraffin when you stuck your head in?"

"No. Not that I remember. Mind you, it can't have been more than a second before I was laid out."

"If you had *smelled* it, you'd have

remembered. And I can't think you'd miss it. It was very strong. All right then, Sam. That tells us one or two things about your attacker."

"I suppose you're going to tell me what they are, Henry?"

"Yes. He broke the window at the side before you got there, but he broke the others *after* he'd clobbered you. So being interrupted didn't put him off his stroke. He tipped the paraffin out *after* he'd clobbered you as well. At least, it looks that way to me.

"And that's all he did, Sam. The paraffin and the windows. But what would he have done if you *hadn't* disturbed him? That's the question. I think he was going to fire the place, Sam. I can't imagine that he'd tip the paraffin out and let it drain away. And although stones don't burn, all the rest of our stuff in The Fortress would have burned. Including the roof spars. So, when you think about it, Sam, you probably saved me from having to build the roof all over again."

"And if he'd fired the place, I might be dead," Sam added, shrewdly.

"My point exactly, Sam. Our man's obviously prepared to do damage, but he stopped short at the risk of burning you.

"He isn't prepared to kill."

15

SAM LITTLE was advised to convalesce for at least three weeks and — acting as Sam's conscience — Henry forbade him to leave his cottage. But Henry visited the old man frequently, spending more time at Sam's cottage than he spent at Eden. Not a single day passed, however, in which he failed to find some time to check over the plot.

Whoever was responsible for the damage, it seemed they were working a five-day week. Once again, nothing happened over Saturday and Sunday, which was a blessing.

Henry wondered if fear had driven them away.

They must be aware that their attack on Sam was potentially very serious and perhaps that knowledge had pressured them into ending their campaign of disruption. It was a happy notion, but after a moment's thought he rejected it wholly. The hope of finding true conscience in people who would strike down an old man was a slender thread indeed.

Henry believed they would be back. And he was right.

By Sunday evening he had replaced the burned fence with a new section in stove-enamelled metal, fitted with a heavy gate and a security padlock, and when he left Eden the place was in rare good order.

He came back on Monday evening to chaos.

His favourite rose-bushes had been split and hacked to pieces, apparently with an axe; the pile of accumulated timber and building material beside The Fortress had been scattered far and wide and half of its contents were missing; his wooden bench-seat had been overturned and tossed into the heart of the reed-bed and the door of The Fortress had been wrenched off and split into several pieces.

During the remainder of that week, incidents continued to occur with increasing intensity. His foot-bridges were wrecked in turn, and when he rebuilt them they were wrecked again. His fence was ripped out and twisted out of shape. Growing plants were plucked out and scattered among the reeds and his wheel-barrow vanished, never to be found again.

For lack of fittings, Henry had not reglazed the windows of The Fortress and in retrospect he was glad, because intruders smashed furniture and scattered tools and he felt certain that if there had been glass in the windows, that too would have been destroyed.

By week-end, Henry was beside himself with rage and impotence. He no longer made any attempt to repair the ravages his enemies created.

The discovery of his dinghy, holed and half-submerged, was the last straw. That was the sight which greeted him on the Monday evening following yet another undisturbed week-end. He dragged the craft ashore and inverted it, but his patience was exhausted and he worked in a red haze of rage, determined somehow to put an end to the cowardly attacks.

Sam would not be about for two more weeks, so Henry could take risks without involving Sam. In spite of the weight and frequency of damage, he still considered it would be unwise to take his problem to the police.

But he could — and would — be his own policeman.

* * *

The pattern of attacks on Eden was as clear now as it would ever be. They were day-time happenings.

The perpetrators had kept a close watch on him over a period. They knew they could expect to find him at Eden, each evening and all the week-end. But he never went there during the working day, so they knew it was safe then to do their dirty work. Once he had worked their system out, it called for no particular guile on Henry's part to devise a plan for beating them at their own game.

He stopped at a call-box on the way home.

No use calling Mr Tomlinson, the senior partner, since he was in Brussels on some jaunt or other and only due to arrive back in time to start work on Tuesday morning. And Henry certainly wasn't going to speak to either of the juniors on such a personal matter. So that seemed to leave only one alternative. He looked up a number and dialled it. She answered promptly.

"Good evening, Miss Dawkins," he told her.

"Mr Crumblestone. It's you." She sounded flustered.

"Yes. I've rung up to ask if you'll do me a favour."

"A favour? What is it?"

"Quite simple, Miss Dawkins. Speak

to Mr Tomlinson in the morning. Tell him I won't be in."

"You mean you'll be late for work, Mr Crumblestone?"

"Not late, no. I mean I won't be in at all tomorrow."

"Oh!" There was a short pause. Then: — "He's bound to ask me what's the reason. What shall I tell him?"

"Tell him I've got a personal problem. A bereavement."

"Oh! I'm sorry to hear that, Mr Crumblestone."

He chuckled, and the sound rang in her ears.

"That's just a little white lie, Miss Dawkins," he placated. "So don't be sorry. If Mr Tomlinson asks for a reason, give him that one. I'll put him right later and pull his leg about it."

* * *

Leaving the call-box he smiled at his own thoughts.

176

He had never involved his secretary before in quite that way. She'd be all of a dither, poor girl, wondering what he was up to. But he could be certain of one thing. She'd do as he asked, and she'd do it convincingly.

He had made a note of her number on the corner of the directory-cover. Now he tore off the corner and carefully put it in his wallet. He drove home with a scheme simmering in his mind and put the finishing touches to it in bed, just before falling asleep.

★ ★ ★

Next morning, he followed a routine pattern.

He rose and prepared for work as usual, took Joan her morning cup of coffee in bed and shouted 'good-bye, dear' as he left the house.

Once clear of the house, he turned away from Wiscliffe and followed a roundabout route along side lanes which brought him near to the entrance of the Wiscliffe Heron Angling Club. From there he drove on an occupational road which led eventually to Plattsford Bridge, but a quarter of a mile short of the bridge he parked in a cut-off beside the road and completed the journey on foot.

The tricky bit was entering Eden itself.

At that time of morning, traffic was flowing briskly, and he wanted to avoid being seen, since he had no way of knowing if the vandals came by car. He hid himself behind the stonework on the upstream side of the bridge and waited for a quiet spell. Then he crossed the bridge, peered over the downstream parapet, satisfied himself there was nobody in sight and climbed over the parapet. He dropped among the rank grass at the foot of the bridge.

He was inside.

After a pause, he crept stealthily towards the river's edge, passing behind The Fortress and down the slope until he came to a thick patch of familiar elders. He wormed his way into the heart of the bushes and settled to wait.

It was prickly and cramped in there, and in many ways The Fortress would have been more comfortable. But Henry reasoned that if intruders came they would check The Fortress first, before showing their hand. They would never think of looking under the bushes.

Added to which, the place he had chosen was an excellent point of vantage. He could see virtually the whole of Eden from there — could command a view of the River Wissey itself to a point well beyond the alien preserves of the Wiscliffe Yachting Marina and Caravan Club. By rising to crooked legs he could pick out the Marina's chain-link fence from end to end. Indeed, with the exception of a small, unimportant area shielded from his sight by the dark cube of The Fortress, no part of the plot was safe from his eyes.

As far as he could make out, no fresh damage had been caused overnight. So if they were coming, they had not arrived yet, and Henry had a head start. The same point added strength to his theory that the marauders played their mischief during the day. Let them come and do so on this occasion and discovery would be inevitable.

The day was warm, but time dragged painfully.

As morning advanced towards noon and noon gave way to a slowly waning sun, Henry began to fear that his plan would fail. He had miscalculated in some particular. Motor vehicles had been zipping over the bridge all day, but none had stopped or even slowed. He had seen the occasional pedestrian walking on the road, but none had shown more than casual interest in Eden.

What could possibly have gone wrong?

Henry found it impossible to believe that the vandals had simply ceased to operate. For weeks now, they had come daily without fail. No manner of logic would allow that they had cried halt — still less that such a decision had precisely coincided with the day of Henry's vigil. They would certainly come.

Wouldn't they?

As the day wore on, Henry's confidence became a sickly parody of its earlier self. He was about to fail — and there had to be some reason for failure. Perhaps his cover was less effective than he fondly imagined? Perhaps even now, some evil-minded destroyer was watching Henry and prudently staying his hand?

Henry looked carefully about him and at once dismissed that possibility. It didn't make sense. The concealing elders were thick with leaf and blossom and — even looking outwards from within — it was difficult to see clearly between the foliage. It simply wasn't possible that someone out yonder — even someone equipped with binoculars or some similar artificial aid — could have a better view inwards. No. They couldn't actually *see* him. Henry felt certain of that.

But suppose they knew he was there? Perhaps he'd been less than careful in taking up position? Whoever the vandals were, he already knew they kept a careful watch on Eden. Wasn't it reasonable to suppose that they'd been there this very morning? There ahead of Henry, to witness his surreptitious entry?

If so, then at this very minute they must be picturing him, crouched among damp bushes with his clothing invaded by ants and spiders, and be laughing their silly heads off.

Suddenly, that seemed a very probable answer.

Henry crimsoned with shame as he allowed his reasoning to develop into firm belief. Whoever 'they' were, they'd beaten him at his own game and must now be making a meal of the joke.

Well, he'd give them no more amusement. He'd rise with as much dignity as he could muster, bring this farce to an end and skulk off home to dream up another plan.

16

BUT it is often when the gas seems to have gone out that the milk boils over.

Henry was in the act of rising from cramped haunches when something large and brightly coloured intruded, right on the edge of his field of vision, as though suddenly projected on a cine-screen.

Hastily he ducked down and turned his head to peer through the branches. The object was a motor launch and it was emerging from the nearest arch of Plattsford Bridge. He recognised the craft at once. Jenks' launch. Or the one he seemed to use at any rate. And as on the earlier occasion it was drifting slowly down the Wissey with engine stilled, hugging the near bank and seeming so close that Henry might have reached out and touched it.

Rising cautiously to his feet, he craned his neck for a better view. He could see the figure standing at the helm and it was unmistakably that of Jenks. The man's body seemed to threaten by its very size. His brick-red face was exactly as Henry had seen it before, round and objectionable. Jenks was frowning in a fixed way, as though the frown were the natural state of his features in repose. Even now, when he was presumably out to enjoy himself, Jenks could not look happy.

Henry kept an alert eye on the boat as it drifted, and on Jenks as he stood regally immobile. It was as though this were an action replay of an earlier event, except that this time Jenks was alone. The man Finch was not with him.

But Jenks alone was amply sufficient to the day.

In his heart, Henry had always suspected that the culprit would prove to be this man, and he felt fiercely grateful that his suspicions had been confirmed.

Ever since their first encounter, months before, he had categorised Jenks as a vindictive and malicious individual with a hot temper and a supremely selfish attitude, who would derive much satisfaction from undoing the work of others. Yet it was inconceivable that even Jenks would do these things for nothing. He had to have a reason, and Henry could only guess what that reason might be.

But Jenks was the one all right.

The evidence pointing to Jenks might be entirely circumstantial, but it was strong, and Henry had no qualms about reaching a decision on the strength of it.

But it began to seem now that his decision was premature. The launch continued to drift downriver and Jenks stayed stubbornly at the helm. Even when the launch drew level with Henry's jetty, the man made no move. It had begun to appear that he had no intention of coming ashore. And if he didn't come ashore . . . ? Well, he could hardly wreak havoc from his boat.

So Henry had evidently completely misread the signs.

More than that, he had seriously wronged the man Jenks, by harbouring all those totally unjustified suspicions. He felt saddened and mortified. There had been no call to label Jenks with all those adjectives he had savoured in his mind. Unpleasant he might be, but Jenks was not a villain.

He'd made another mistake too — because Jenks was not alone. Almost as though he had been hidden there, Frank Finch rose into view in the boat's well and shuffled his way to the stern, where he leaned against the coaming as Henry had seen him once before. But it meant nothing. In a sense, it doubled Henry's guilt, because in damning Jenks he had included Finch as the other half of a brace of blackguards.

The launch drifted past Lake Ceylon and onwards until it had completely cleared the limits of Eden.

About then there was a splutter and a roar as the engine of the launch sprang to life and at once Jenks began to steer into the mouth of the Marina's entrance channel. Henry could read nothing but propriety into that manoeuvre.

Effectively, he had final confirmation of his own misjudgment. Jenks and Finch had been out for a run on the river — a perfectly lawful outing — and it had ended as lawfully as it must have begun.

To Henry's surprise, the launch stopped.

He had expected it to continue along the channel until it disappeared somewhere in the heart of the Marina, instead of which it came to rest with its stern still jutting out into the river.

On the far side of the Marina's channel there was a strip of walk-board fitted parallel with the bank and lined with buffers made from old car-tyres. Henry knew it was there — he had seen it in use at week-ends as temporary mooring — but he had not expected Jenks to moor there, or to step ashore as soon as the launch butted alongside. Nevertheless, that was exactly what Jenks did, and he was carrying the end of a rope, which trailed behind him.

Henry felt a flicker of re-awakened interest.

Frank Finch crossed the well of the launch and followed Jenks ashore. Finch too, carried the end of a rope, and it seemed they proposed to tie-up fore and aft. As if to confirm Henry's reading of the signs, Jenks bore his rope forrard and lashed the launch's bow to a stump. He then strolled aft and took possession of the second rope from Finch.

And the second rope completely changed the picture.

Taking a firm stance on the walk-way, Jenks began to haul in the second rope, and as it began to tighten it became obvious that it was not attached to the launch, but to something upstream.

189

Gripped now by fascination, Henry kept his eyes on the rope as it rose dripping from the water, its dark length running parallel with the river bank towards Plattsford Bridge. For a mad second or two, he conjured all kinds of weird notions to explain Jenks' curious behaviour. Murder had been done and the body would shortly appear at the end of the tightening rope; or bigger fish swam in the Wissey than Henry had ever realised and Jenks was tackled up for them; or Jenks was a smuggler, a drug-peddlar, a fence, and the rope was shackled to some monstrous example of the stuff of his trade.

Careless of concealment now, Henry stood up and poked head and shoulders out from the bushes. He followed the rope upstream with his eyes until its last dangling coil was bared.

The rope was tied to Henry's jetty.

Even then, he was slow to realise the significance of the rope. The situation seemed ridiculous by any reckoning. What possible purpose could Jenks have in tying his launch to Henry's jetty on such a long lead? Did he hope to pass something along the rope? And if so, what? Or was it his purpose to haul the launch upriver, stern first? And if so, Why?

The answer came rapidly.

As Henry watched and wondered, Jenks braced himself and yanked hard on the tightened rope. He spoke to Finch over his shoulder and Finch joined him at the haul. There sounded the ominous creaking of timbers under stress and the end spar of Henry's jetty splintered and broke free. Jenks had calculated nicely in choosing that spar. It had borne much of the weight of the jetty, which now sank alarmingly at its lower end and buried its leading edge beneath the surface of the water.

Jenks was grinning widely now. He had some conversation with Finch and Finch also grinned. Then, like a trawlerman at his nets, Jenks hauled on the rope hand over hand and dragged the spar ashore.

Henry was incensed.

"You swine, Jenks," he shouted, leaping into full view and war-dancing among the reeds. "That was a deliberate act. You'll pay for that you rotten hound. I'll sue for damages."

The big man was taken aback at Henry's sudden appearance, but seemed unimpressed by his threats.

"Ooops, sorry!" he shouted, a crafty grin on his face. Then he addressed Finch. "Didn't know we were trailing a rope, Frank. Looks as though it got tangled up with the man's jetty."

Finch sniggered but said nothing.

"You'll be sorry all right," Henry mouthed. "By the time I've finished with you, you'll wish you'd never seen this place."

But Jenks dismissed him with an airy wave of his hand.

"Have it your own way," he shouted. "I've told you it was a sheer accident. If you think I did it on purpose, you must be sick in your mind. Here — have your bloody stump back."

So saying, Jenks heaved the spar upwards and outwards.

It sailed through the air twisting end over end, landed in mid-river with a smacking splash and began to drift away downstream. Then, as though the business had been concluded to everyone's satisfaction, Jenks and Finch climbed back aboard the launch and headed inshore along the channel.

There was nothing more to say. Henry stood speechless.

★ ★ ★

Minutes later he composed a torrent of well-phrased threats and insults which he would have loved to hurl at Jenks and Finch, but they had disappeared by then, and it was too late. Henry could only stand in helpless indignation, watching the jetty-spar as it drifted from his sight.

And then — even in the height of his wrath — it occurred to Henry that if he worked quickly he could salvage something from the mess, if only the spar. His dinghy lay upturned on the shore, holed and useless, but he still had the punt.

The thought galvanized him into action.

Stepping across the sagging jetty he unhitched the punt and climbed inboard, reaching for the paddle.

He felt the water at once, swilling about his shoes, and before the craft was clear of the jetty it began to sink slowly under his weight.

Hastily he grabbed the planks of the jetty and hauled himself ashore, lifting the prow of the punt behind him. There was a sucking, gurgling sound as water sluiced along the well of the punt and the cause of the trouble came into view.

A yard from the prow and right on the waterline, there was a hole. It was newly cut and jagged.

It had obviously been made with an axe.

Henry Crumblestone was shattered in spirit. Crushed.

Sadly he clambered from the steeply sloping jetty, walked along the main and central gravel path, crossed two footbridges and headed for his car, passing all the poor symbols of his occupation along the way.

Reaching the new metal fence — still in position and undamaged after two whole days — he let himself out and carefully locked the gate behind him. Then he turned and leaned on the fence, taking a long look at the place which had once been a wilderness of marsh and reeds but which now — in spite of so many cruel set-backs — had the look of a pleasure ground.

The dream had been quite beautiful.

Potentially, the reality was more beautiful still, but he would enjoy it no more. The concerted efforts of the forces of evil, in the shape of Basil Jenks and his gnome-like accomplice, would not allow him to enjoy it.

And all the fight was gone out of him, dissipated by the latest round of the battle, which had gone so convincingly to Jenks. Jenks would certainly keep the pressure up, and Henry had lost the will to resist. So he would capitulate.

The decision was firmly made.

He would walk away from this little corner of peace and plenty — and never come back.

17

THE dream was over, and a sleepless night did nothing to alleviate Henry's mood of utter dejection.

Indeed, had it not been for the timely intervention of Mary Dawkins, his secretary, Henry Crumblestone might never have recovered his will.

It was the morning following his final brush with Jenks. Sitting in his office, he was silent and morose and for once Mary's bright prattle and friendly attention failed to dispel his gloom. He forced a smile in response to her cheery "*Good morning, Mr Crumblestone,*" but thereafter he felt quite unable to appreciate her light-hearted comments about the weather, the state of the nation or her plans for the forthcoming summer holidays. He dealt with correspondence in a desultory manner, obviously preoccupied with other thoughts.

Mary noticed at once.

She could not help but notice, and she grew more and more concerned. She withheld comment until she had served the morning coffee and then she drew up a chair beside him and patted him on the shoulder.

"Something's troubling you, Mr Crumblestone," she accused.

"Eh?" He looked up at her and shook a weary head. "No, it's nothing Miss Dawkins. I'll be well enough in a little while."

"I've waited a while already," she persisted. "You're just as sad-looking now as when I first arrived. Won't you tell me what's the matter and if there's anything I can do to help?"

"No. It's nothing. Please leave me alone."

She rose dutifully and carried the tray away while Henry made another futile attempt to concentrate on his work. Fifteen minutes or so passed in silence and then she tried again.

"Look, Mr Crumblestone. You can't go on like this. Are you sure you aren't sickening for something? You'll have to shake it off, you know. Buck up, sir. Nothing can be as bad as all that."

But it could — and Henry knew it could.

So many things had happened to him lately, and they had all been that bad. In the end, everything was that bad.

There had been good things too, of course.

He had been supremely happy not so long ago, building up a haven for himself in the loveliest of settings, and if events had worked out in other ways he might have gone on being happy. But happiness had come to an end. His venture had failed. He had lost Eden. And it was all as bad as that.

Henry no longer felt able to bear the load of adversity which had so unfairly accrued. So he would try to forget it. It didn't please him to have Mary Dawkins reminding him of it. He fended her concern with half-hearted reassurances and all the while his thoughts kept returning to the morass of his disillusionment.

But Mary was determined to cheer him up.

By persistence, she made a little progress. Gradually, Henry relinquished his stand of complete disinterest and began to consider the problem from an opposite point of view. Here he was, thinking solely about Eden, when he really ought to be considering the broader canvas.

He had been driven away from a cherished facility, but did it follow that his life was in ruins? Nothing of the sort! In the end, he was no worse off, without Eden, than he had been before. In fact, arguably he was better off, because he had enjoyed Eden for several months and to that extent he could lay claim to success. Besides, in walking away from the mess as he had done, he had brought with him a rich store of happy memories. Mary

Dawkins would appreciate sentiments like that. She'd stop harping at him if she knew.

He felt an irresistible urge to tell her everything.

So far he had never told the truth about Eden to a living soul, for fear the word might spread and spark off unwanted consequences. Now the episode was over — killed stone dead — so it no longer mattered. There would be no real value in telling Mary Dawkins, but there would be no harm in it either.

And he wanted to tell her.

"Sit down, Miss Dawkins," he told her. "I want you to listen to a story.

* * *

The dredging of his memory and the re-discovery of half-forgotten hopes had a profound effect on Henry. He began his story as though from the standpoint of a returned voyager, speaking of matters which once had been and were now history, but as the story unfolded he became increasingly aware that the past was still with him, and perhaps it could be moulded into some sort of worthwhile future.

By the time his story ended he was animated and voluble, describing urgent problems as part of the present and making plans for overcoming them.

Mary Dawkins listened, gravely attentive, the work of the office shelved and forgotten. When she had heard everything she gave the advice he had expected her to give.

"Tell the police. Mr Crumblestone. You must."

"That's easier said than done, Miss Dawkins," he demurred. "It's a case of 'the devil you know' I'm afraid. If this were happening at home — or here in the office — I'd be on the blower like a shot. But I daren't do it. I have no right to be on that land in the first place."

Her response took him completely off guard.

"Who says so?"

"Who says so?" he echoed uncertainly. "Well, I do, to begin with."

"I know that. But who else?"

He considered the question in silence. Then:-

"Nobody else, I suppose. Not the Marina. And certainly not Jenks, or he'd have said so — and he'd have taken great pleasure in kicking me off. But give him his due, Jenks has never laid claim to the place, for all he'd love to scare me away by his dirty tactics."

"All right, then." There was a hint of triumph in her voice which Henry knew to be totally misplaced. "You're a solicitor, Mr Crumblestone. You must know something about rights. In this sort of case, where the land doesn't have an owner, can't you make some sort of claim to it? I seem to have read somewhere that you can."

He nodded sympathetically.

"Yes — but it won't work. In the long run, it is possible to gain what's known as 'Adverse Title' by staying in possession. But it takes a minimum of twelve years. And you've got to understand that for the whole of that twelve year period I'd be at the mercy of the true owner, who could turn me off at a minute's notice. Even if I refused to go, he could enforce his rights in next to no time, just by applying for a Court Order."

"But there isn't an owner."

"Oh come, Miss Dawkins. There isn't any such thing as land without an owner. If you thought I said that, I must have misled you. There has to be an owner somewhere."

"All right, Mr Crumblestone. Let's suppose there is. If you knew who it was, you'd hand the land straight back to him?"

"Of course. I'd have no real option. But I wouldn't want to keep it anyway, in those circumstances."

Mary Dawkins beamed confidently.

"There you are, then," she said. "And at the present, nobody seems to be worrying about it, except you. I think you've got more rights than you believe, Mr Crumblestone. I say that land is yours until somebody shows up who has a better claim. When that happens, you must leave the place at once, but *until it happens* I can see no reason on earth why you shouldn't carry on using the place. And what's more, in spite of what you say, I don't think the police would have the slightest grumble about that."

"I'm sorry Miss Dawkins, but I can't go to the police," he insisted. "They'd check up straight away and find out that I was a trespasser."

"I don't think they'd do anything of the kind. Why should they? Where would they check? And on whose behalf? I've heard you say it yourself Mr Crumblestone, more than once. You can't be a trespasser until somebody says you're trespassing."

The girl was talking good sense and Henry knew it.

This time, when he smiled, there was

nothing forced about the look.

"That's a good point," he allowed. "However, I'm still not inclined to involve the police."

"All right then — don't. But don't move out, either. Stick to your guns Mr Crumblestone. You mustn't let that horrible man Jenks drive you away from land he doesn't own. You must go back there and fight him."

"Fight him?" he grinned. "Have you seen the size of him?"

She smiled as La Giaconda must have smiled before da Vinci's brush and her thoughts went lofting far away.

"Yes. Fight him. I don't mean physically, and I don't mean any sort of tit-for-tat by returning his dirty tricks. But fight him just by staying there. By refusing to let him run you out, no matter how unpleasant he tries to make things for you. You'll find the ways, Mr Crumblestone."

"Half an hour ago, I'd written the whole thing off," he mused. "I'm not so sure now. If I knew why Jenks was doing these things it would help."

She appraised him and her look held something of scorn.

"You know very well why," she said. "It's because he wants you to leave. And if you *do* leave, you'll be playing everything his way. And there's something else too," she added darkly. "If you do move out, I shouldn't be in the least surprised to see Jenks move in. After all the work you've done there, you don't want to let him have it as part of his wretched Marina."

Henry Crumblestone was animated. He beamed.

The resolve to go back to Eden and enjoy it to the full, in spite of Jenks and the worst he might do, filled Henry's soul to bursting.

Also, he was seeing Mary Dawkins from a completely fresh angle, and what he saw filled him with admiration. He had been completely won over by her advocacy and he had found unexpected support in the intensity of her spirit.

"And, Mr Crumblestone . . . " she went on.

"Yes, Miss Dawkins."

"I like the sound of Eden. When you've managed to get everything nice and tidy up there, I'd love to visit and see it for myself."

"So you shall, Miss Dawkins," he promised. "So you shall."

18

FIRED with enthusiasm and spurred to fresh endeavour, Henry began again. He spent a deal of time and energy in Eden, making good the damage to his property.

He missed the advice and assistance of Sam Little.

Although Sam's wound had healed remarkably well, his age was a factor against rapid return to health and his Doctor advised complete rest. Sam was not the resting kind, and Henry was obliged to bully him into compliance. Sam stayed grudgingly at home, and as part of the deal, Henry drove the old man to Plattsford Bridge each Saturday to spend half an hour viewing Eden from the warmth and comfort of Henry's car.

Those short periods apart, Henry

spent his time in solitude and happy drudgery.

Repairing the jetty was no easy task. Before he could attempt it, he needed a new spar of just the right size and quality, and the procurement of such an item was more difficult than he had imagined it would be. Moreover, spring had melted into summer and summer was fighting a losing battle against the advancement of chilly autumn. The evenings were very short now, and standing scantily clad, up to his waist in water, was a shivery and uncomfortable business which Henry could only tolerate for short periods.

But he persisted, and in the course of a couple of weeks he restored the jetty to wholeness. He even added several extra cross-members to provide strength, so that the finished job was a distinct improvement on the old.

He completely refurbished The Fortress: cleaned up the mess inside; replaced broken furniture and tools; mended the door, adding a new lock and re-fitting the finished article on fresh hinges; re-glazed the windows and expended a fresh mixing of mortar to stop up cracks between the stones.

Next he turned his attention to the damaged boats.

His dinghy was holed in two places, but some careful plugging with fibreglass and cement rendered it watertight. The punt, though, was much more of a problem, calling for a new section of timber and a great deal of patching and caulking, but Henry borrowed a manual on boat-building and learned enough wrinkles to produce a workmanlike finish.

After that, he tidied up the garden beds; fashioned and erected a new notice-board which he lodged in concrete; bolted a flat metal plate to the fence and inscribed the name 'Eden' upon it; replaced his wooden bench, incinerator and litter bins; imported fresh stocks of fuel for the stove and pressure lamp in The Fortress and then sat back with tingling nerves to await the next reprisal.

But it seemed that Jenks and Finch had learned their lesson. There were no further outbreaks of damage. On more than one occasion Henry saw the pair, either cruising on the river aboard their launch or skulking on Marina land beyond the chain-link fence. But whenever they appeared, Henry chose to ignore them, and they seemed happy to return the silent antipathy, which suited Henry very well.

October arrived, bearing a short Indian summer.

The late sun found Eden in first class order and Henry was once more able to dawdle and spend his time strolling through the property he had come to call his own. He walked the river-bank in undisturbed enjoyment, admiring the scene, prying into corners, reading the signs of nature in water and willow and telling himself that there would be some good winter fishing to be had in Eden, ere long.

It was a period of mellow consolidation. A grand finale to the season's growth. The earth reached full ripeness and flaunted its abundance in the face of encroaching decay.

And the chub moved back into Lake Ceylon.

★ ★ ★

Which was a minor miracle in Henry's eyes.

Weeks before, when he had first become certain that the chub were gone, he had thought it a temporary migration and had looked for their reappearance daily. But when so much time passed and there were no signs of the fish he began to fear that they had left him for ever — and gradually the fear crystallised into certainty.

Now, magically, they were back.

It was rather like the appearance of fat buds on a plant supposedly dead, and as one would come upon such manifestations of life, he discovered the return of the chub by accident.

For more than an hour that evening, he had been sitting on the downstream edge of his jetty, stret-pegging with light tackle and using bread-flake bait. The fish were on, and his keep-net bulged with good quality roach and bream.

But a lull had come upon him — no strange occurrence in such circumstances — and his porcupine-quill float rode all but motionless, its red point tipping the surface of the water and forming its characteristic 'V' of turbulence. For some reason best known to themselves the fish had gone off feed, might even have moved away completely for all the attention they were giving him.

Henry accepted the lull stoically.

The fish must have become sated, he supposed, by the liberal helpings of groundbait he had fed them. So they would fast for a while. He had time now for relaxation and contemplation.

Lake Ceylon lay inland to Henry's

left front and it was visible as a calm, silver patch amid waving tendrils of dark green rushes. The Marina's chain-link fence bordered the pool on its far side. The fence was an ugly thing in every respect, but in view of the effect it had had on his life, Henry had grown inordinately fond of the feature.

In the early days the fence had been stark and bare, an incongruity to mar a sylvan setting, but since then in her inimitable way, Nature had been working to heal the scar. Fresh clumps of reed and grass had established themselves in the soil at the foot of the fence, while trailing creepers of wild-rose, bramble and thorn had also appeared, twining themselves about the concrete posts and in and out the diamond meshes. At this rate, the fence would soon be thoroughly and prettily overgrown, and Henry rejoiced that it was so.

Leaving the fence, he moved his scrutiny inwards until his eyes rested on the dead Lake Ceylon. And in that instant, like a breaking mirror, the pool's surface was distorted by a dimple and a widening circle of tiny waves.

A rise!

It was a very small rise indeed, and within seconds the small pool had reverted to glassy stillness, but a fish had shown itself and Henry was alert and tingling. Of course it was probably a bleak or a small dace. Nothing to get excited about. But it would do no harm to explore the event.

Henry broke a few small pieces from a crust of bread and flicked them towards the pool.

The distance was too great for accuracy and several pieces fell short, but two or three tempting morsels landed lightly on the water and began sailing slowly outwards in the direction of the main river. Henry watched them with stilled breath, watched them as keenly as a trout enthusiast would have watched drifting mayflies.

One piece of crust in particular,

found a speedier current and within half a minute it had sailed the length of the pool, swirled momentarily at the pool's tail and twisted away downriver. Henry's eyes covered every inch of its journey.

Nothing!

A second piece floated towards the river and seemed about to escape also. But no! Right at the tail of the pool there was a ripple and an audible slurp and the fragment of crust was gone in a frame of widening ripples.

Two further fragments had lodged themselves among reed stems at the far edge of the pool and Henry transferred his gaze to them. Both disappeared simultaneously. And more significantly, Henry *saw* the feeding fish.

There was no mistaking their species. Twin pairs of great white rubbery lips broke the surface alongside the fragments and, with the grace and timing of a chorus-line, two fine chub ate and departed.

Henry had seen enough.

Feverishly he reeled in his tackle, took off float and shot and replaced the size-fourteen hook with one twice as big. He impaled a cube of crust, swung the baited hook outwards and tensed with anticipation as it landed with a plop in the heart of Lake Ceylon.

White, fleshy lips appeared as if by magic. There was a suck and a swirl and Henry's rod arched as it took the strain of a good fish.

It was a two-pounder at least, and it meant to fight. His gossamer line was hardly strong enough and the overhanging vegetation was a severe handicap, making it difficult to keep the fish in open water. But Henry rose to a crouch and concentrated, struggling to keep it away from snags.

Standing twenty yards away, within the grounds of the Marina, Basil Jenks and Frank Finch pressed their faces against the fence and watched the struggle. Henry was much too busy to notice them, until Jenks loosed his sneering shout.

"What's that? A bloody salmon?"

He accompanied his words with a guffaw and Frank Finch, standing at his elbow, added his titter to the general din. Henry heard, but he said nothing.

So Jenks tried again.

"Fancy that, Frank. How stupid can you get? A grown man, drowning bloody worms."

"A worm on one end and a fool on the t'other," Finch contributed.

Picking up their comments with half an ear, Henry smiled quietly to himself and continued to wrestle with the chub.

"You'd catch a hell of a lot more with a hand-grenade," Jenks needled. "That's if you ever wanted more of those stinking bloody things."

Henry was becoming a little irritated.

"Why don't you go and sail your boat, Jenks?" he snapped with a rare show of rudeness. "If I want to catch fish, I shall . . . Blast!"

The inevitable had happened. The darting fish had run headlong into the

219

main body of reeds and there was a faint *ping* as Henry's line parted. Jenks saw, heard and *knew*.

"Can't catch fish for bloody toffee," he chortled. "I've seen a little lad with a bent pin do better than that."

And he and Frank Finch dissolved in a flood of jeering laughter.

For a short moment, Henry watched their performance straight-faced. Then he turned away and began slowly to dismantle his rod and pack his tackle away for the evening.

Let them laugh, he told himself. He cared nothing for such ignorance. And if they believed for an instant that losing the fish had upset Henry, they were stupidly wide of the mark.

Henry's heart was full of joy. He was happier than he had been for ages. Because Lake Ceylon was back in business.

Those great, fat, hungry chub had come home.

19

IT was undiluted joy.

Joy in a form too cloying for one man to handle, for unlike most tangible commodities, joy increases with the sharing. Man is seldom taught that fact, but he knows it by instinct, virtually from birth.

Henry Crumblestone needed to share his joy.

To some extent, Sam Little satisfied the need. The old man was mending rapidly now and with Henry's help he managed to spend an hour or two each week, sitting in The Fortress or stumping round Eden in Henry's wake. He pried and rooted into everything and the edge of his curiosity never seemed a whit dulled.

Come the following spring, Sam frequently threatened, Henry would have to watch out. Because Sam would be bidding to take the place over. Especially the fishing.

And Henry's joy grew in consequence, but still there was room in his heart for more. The re-birth of Lake Ceylon following so closely on the resurrection of Eden itself, had captured his enthusiasm, and like a child with a fresh plaything he was agog for an audience.

But he was a cautious man too.

He considered long and carefully before inviting Mary Dawkins to visit Eden. Next to Sam, she was the one person he most wanted to see there. What was more, she had asked to see the place. She genuinely wanted to come to Eden, and that made the prospect of her visit all the more important and pleasurable. Besides, hadn't he made her a firm promise?

But to set against that, there was Joan.

The problem of Joan was technical rather than emotional. She was more of a business partner than a wife, and if Henry's interest in her was material, hers in him was wholly financial. Not since the first year of their marriage had they gone out together or lived a mutually sharing existence like any normal married couple.

To give her due credit, Joan seldom objected to his own wanderings and he was grateful for that — but not for an instant did Henry delude himself that his wife would countenance even the most platonic association between himself and another woman.

Her own shenanigans were not a considered criterion, however much they ought to have been. Undoubtedly she was playing away from home with some other man — with a whole boiling of other men, perhaps — but she would never condone such activity on Henry's part. The moment the slightest breath of scandal reached Joan's ears the heavens would tumble on his head — and Joan in high wrath was too fearful a proposition to contemplate.

The situation was ridiculous. Disturbing

too, if one's deeper emotions happened to be involved, but knowing of her faithlessness impressed Henry so little that he was hardly curious. There were plaster saints, he supposed, but Joan was not among their number. He could no longer be hurt by her attitude. He even found it amusing in a perverse way.

And whatever the outcome, he would run the risk of Joan's wrath. Because he had assured Mary Dawkins that he would take her to visit Eden. So visit Eden she would.

The matter had been in his mind for some days but it emerged as a decision that evening as he drove homeward, warm with the memory of the chub.

Early afternoon would probably be the most suitable time, he reasoned. Joan did her shopping in the morning as regularly as a habit, and each afternoon she usually rested. Late evening was the time she really came alive, and the chances of finding her out before then were slim.

It would mean taking time off work, but he was well enough established in business to be able to arrange leave more or less at will — and since the sole duty Mary Dawkins had was to act personally for him, it followed that she could be spared also.

Once he had taken the idea, warmed and shaped it, he felt confident the thing could be done that way. And the sooner the better.

In fact — why not tomorrow?

He broached the subject as soon as she arrived at the office on the following day and Mary was plainly enthusiastic.

"But we'll have to be careful," he counselled her.

"Careful?" she queried, looking puzzled.

He grinned weakly, pink with embarrassment.

"Yes. After all Miss Dawkins, I'm a married man. It would never do for people to start thinking the wrong things. Especially my wife."

"Oh, Mr Crumblestone!" she exclaimed, colouring.

"Yes, I know it's all so silly. But you know how nosy people can sometimes be. The less they see, the better."

Mary Dawkins was discomfited and unhappy.

"But Mr Crumblestone," she said hollowly, "I really don't think it would look so . . . so . . . And anyway, if it does look that way, I'd rather not bother. I'd like to see Eden, but I don't want to cause . . ."

He stopped her with a raised hand.

"Please don't get all upset about it, Miss Dawkins. Of course you must come. All I ask is that we behave discreetly."

★ ★ ★

They made their way to Eden in separate cars, stealthily, like conspirators in some heinous plan.

And they stumbled by chance on other conspirators.

Henry reached Eden first and would have waited for Mary Dawkins' Mini which was a short distance behind, but in the instant of climbing out of his Rover he realised that something was amiss. Somewhere, very close at hand, he could hear a chugging engine, and when he looked he could see a launch moored at his jetty. It was an all too familiar motor launch and Basil Jenks was aboard it, standing in typical pose.

At first, Henry saw only Jenks, but that was enough to arouse his anger. Forgetting all about his guest, he vaulted over the fence and began to run towards the jetty.

"You clear off from there, Jenks," he shouted angrily as he hurried along the gravel path. "You're not wanted on this land."

It surprised Henry somewhat, to see that Jenks seemed reluctant to move off. He reached and took hold of his mooring rope, but was slow to slip it free. Was he proposing to stay and argue, Henry wondered. Because if he did, there was bound to be an undignified scene.

But there was an explanation, and Henry soon discovered it. He had taken less than a dozen paces towards the jetty when he became aware of a further movement towards his far left and he turned to see a scuttling figure moving riverwards at a crouch. It was a very well known figure.

Frank Finch!

Warned by Henry's cry, Finch had already covered a lot of ground, and before Henry was half-way to the jetty, Finch had scrambled aboard. At once, Jenks slipped his mooring and wound up the engine to a roar. The launch surged away in ignominious retreat.

Henry was beside himself with rage and dismay.

Following their earlier attack on his jetty, when he had caught both Jenks and Finch red-handed, they had left him strictly alone and he had convinced himself that they would go on doing so. Now the destructive scoundrels were operating again, and he had caught them a second time. The sign was an ominous one. He stopped at the first footbridge, shouted and shook his fist after the departing launch.

He was still mouthing unpleasantries when Mary Dawkins joined him.

"Did you see that?" he hurled at her. "That swine Jenks again and his rotten little sidekick. They've been up to something."

"Never mind, Mr Crumblestone," she soothed. "They've gone now. You mustn't let them upset you like this."

And, left like that, Henry might have been mollified, but there was a final thrust to come.

A shrill wolf-whistle sounded and they looked towards the Marina, where the launch was still visible, nosing inland along the channel. The stentorian tones of Basil Jenks reached their ears as plain as a thunderclap.

"Who's the fancy-woman, Crumblestone? She's not your missus — that's for bloody certain."

If Henry was angry, Mary Dawkins was bitterly disappointed.

Her first visit to Eden was to have been a happy occasion, but it had turned sour, and she knew Mr Crumblestone must feel it even more sorely than she did.

Resorting to sympathy, she tried hard to restore Henry's mood, expressed her genuine admiration of the beauty of the plot and showed great enjoyment in strolling about the neat pathways. But Henry's mind was closed to her efforts and he was not appeased.

"They've done something wicked, Miss Dawkins, I know they have," he said bitterly. "That little reptile Finch wasn't here for nothing."

"Maybe you were lucky?" she suggested hopefully. "Whatever they had in mind, you surprised them. They might not have had time to do anything."

"I might just have been early enough,

I suppose," he said more hopefully. "But either way, I've got to find out. Come on, Miss Dawkins. Finch was over yonder beside the fence when I first saw him."

With Mary at his heels, Henry headed inland on a course for the mid-way section of the Marina's chain-link fence. That way, he passed well to the roadward side of Lake Ceylon and came to the embankment, just on his own side of the fence. Here, the small spring that fed the pool emerged from the earth and chuckled over stones on its way along the shallow runnel to its outlet in Lake Ceylon.

This day, it contained more than stones.

There was a green-painted metal container up-ended in the stream and white powder was escaping from it in a steady trickle.

Henry had seen similar containers many times before and knew exactly what it must contain. He snatched it from the water and hurled it aside, but

231

even as he did so he realised he was too late. Most of its contents were already swilling down the tiny stream.

There was no mistaking the look of horror on Henry's face, but as to its cause, Mary could not be certain.

"What is it, Mr Crumblestone?" she asked him apprehensively.

"Cymag." He said. "Deadly poison to fish life."

20

"CAN'T anything be done?" She asked him. But Henry was not listening.

Spurred on by desperation rather than wisdom he had slithered down the course of the little stream and was ripping clods of turf and stones from its banks — piling them across the flow in an attempt to stem the water, and with it, the poison. His purpose was plain to see, and Mary joined him and delved until her arms were blackened.

In rapid style they threw up a sizeable dam which held the water back, producing a small lake above and reducing the stream below to a trickle. But Henry had the stink of failure in his nostrils from the start and after a strenuous ten minutes he straightened up.

"They've beaten us by miles," he

said wretchedly. "Pounds of the stuff must have washed through by now. We're not doing the slightest good by trying to stop the rest."

"And will it kill all your fish?"

"All those that are in its way, yes. Cymag is powerful stuff. It attacks the nervous system, switches off the mechanism they use to breathe. Unless they've had enough sense to skip out and move upstream, where it won't spread. But they won't have done that. Fish don't have that sort of sense unfortunately. Well. Come on, Miss Dawkins. We'd better go and look at the damage."

Lake Ceylon itself was unapproachable from that angle, due to intervening marshy ground, so he hurried round towards the jetty and wormed his way through the reeds until he could look directly into the pool.

Mary followed and stood at his shoulder and together they stared anxiously at the little patch of water. The surface still seemed limpid and clean and for a while it seemed his fears had been without substance. There was a good deal of spongy land between spring and pool, and perhaps in some way the poison had been filtered out before it reached the outlet.

But hope forlorn is cruel, hurting hope.

Mary was first to see the signs. She drew Henry's attention to a swirling movement in the water — not in Lake Ceylon, but in the main river and slightly downstream of the entrance to the pool. Following her pointing finger, Henry was saddened to see three medium-sized chub, drifting belly-up down the river. They had obviously come from Lake Ceylon.

Within a moment of that, they heard wild splashing and saw gouts of reeds beside the pool, swaying and shuddering to the shock of threshing fish. Many more fish were in difficulties, darting and rushing about the pool in a vain attempt to find clean water.

The splashing continued for some

minutes before it eased off to no more than an occasional flurry. At that stage, Henry was dismayed to see two larger chub (in the three to four pound bracket, he thought) darting in slalom out towards the river, flashing their silver sides and gasping and swirling in their death throes.

Fine fish. Too fine to be destroyed in this wanton way. But they were not nearly so fine as another specimen which followed after, still feebly flapping and struggling to right itself. That fish, Henry estimated, must have weighed six pounds or more, and in the course of the next few minutes they saw several other dying fish, almost as large.

Henry had never felt so thwarted and helpless in his life.

The sheer savagery and callousness of Finch's act (and it was the work of Basil Jenks too, he reminded himself) appalled him. He felt like weeping. He also felt extremely angry, but his anger was ice-cold. Controlled.

"Let's get out of here, Miss Dawkins," he said in hollow tones. "I can't stand looking at this."

Mary Dawkins was crying unashamedly. She had none of Henry's affinity with fish, but she had abundant sympathy with all living things and the sight of the dying fish had completely upset her. She felt for Henry too — recognised the crushing blow he must have suffered — and she was filled with compassion.

"Oh, how could they be so cruel?" she wailed. "But you must prosecute this time. What those men have done is a crime, Mr Crumblestone, and you must report it to the police. I'll be your witness. You mustn't let them get away so easily this time."

"It wouldn't do the slightest good," he told her. "It wouldn't save one of those poor, miserable creatures. We're too late for that."

"But you'll do something, surely?"

Henry shook his head ponderously.

"No. There's nothing I can do,

except let nature take its course."

"What does that mean? I'm not sure I follow you."

"Nature heals, to put the thing in its simplest terms," he told her. "And nothing is so serious that it can't be mended — not even this. The saving grace of poison in a river, if the filthy stuff has any saving grace at all, is that it will quickly become diluted. I don't know how much of the stuff they used, but if that can was even half full it'll probably be enough to kill thousands of fish on its way down the river. But it won't kill *all* the fish in the river, not by any means. And that's the point, you see. There'll be plenty of survivors, particularly upstream of here, where the poison will never reach. And when the effects have worn off the remaining fish will re-establish themselves."

"How long will it be before that happens?"

"Before the poison dissipates? Not very long, I think. A few days should do it, if we get some rain to flush the river. And if we don't get rain, well, a couple of weeks at the outside. If you mean how long will it take for the fish stocks to recover, I'd say a good deal longer. It might be years before they're as prolific as they were before."

He seemed to speak almost cheerfully, as though he made little of the incident.

"How can you take it so calmly?" she said, puzzled.

"Calmly?" There was a sudden ring of steel in Henry's voice and his eyes glittered. "Oh but you're quite mistaken, Miss Dawkins. I'm not taking it calmly. Not at all calmly. Let me assure you, it would give me the greatest of pleasure to pump a gallon of that stuff into our nasty friends through a force-feeder. I'm thinking hard about it. For a couple of pence, I'd do it."

"Not you, Mr Crumblestone. You wouldn't do anything so foolish."

"Wouldn't I?" He looked at her and there was a strange light in his eyes, but then his face softened. "Perhaps not.

Anyway, it's time we were leaving. So back to the cars and let us begone."

★ ★ ★

Walking back to the road, Mary had her first real opportunity to see the garden he had carved out of a wilderness. She was tremendously impressed by it, and she dawdled along the way, anxious to see as much of it as possible. But Henry was filled with impatience and he urged her on.

"It's a lovely place, Mr Crumblestone," she said wistfully, standing beside her car and looking back. "I wish I could have stayed longer, to have a proper look round. And it's such a shame that they won't leave you in peace. But you mustn't let them beat you, Mr Crumblestone. No matter what happens, you must stay in this place."

He seemed to look earnestly into her face, but his eyes were distant, as though focussed on the future.

"Jenks can't beat me," he said grimly,

"and he'll find that out before very long. Don't worry, Mary. I haven't finished yet."

* * *

'Mary!'

He had called her by her first name.

Driving back towards Wiscliffe in her Mini, with the red tail-lights of Mr Crumblestone's Rover fading in the distance, she pondered that curious happening.

It was something he had never done before, and she could not help but feel a tiny pang of sadness as she reacted to his change of style.

For years now, for ever it sometimes seemed, she had hoped he would relax in her company enough to drop the stiff and formal 'Miss Dawkins' in favour of the much simpler 'Mary'. First names were so much more friendly somehow — seemed to hold more promise — and it was such a shame that it should only happen now, at the end of a

241

very distressing series of events, when it might indicate no more than strain.

Mr Crumblestone had certainly not been his normal self at the time. In no sense had he used her name warmly, or in a spirit of closer camaraderie. More likely, she supposed, he had called her 'Mary' without conscious thought, merely because that happened to be her name. To him, it probably meant nothing. And that was sad.

Because to Mary it meant a very great deal.

★ ★ ★

Henry did not go directly home.

He went into Wiscliffe first, called at the town's main hardware store and made a bulk purchase.

It was an unusual purchase and the shop assistant seemed startled, but Henry offered no explanation.

Before entering the store, he had emptied the untidy mass of reels, floats, bait-tins and assorted tackle out of his fishing basket into the boot of his car and he took the empty basket with him, assuming it would be big enough to carry the items he purchased.

In the event he was wrong, and he had to use, additionally, two plastic carrier bags purchased from the store. He was fully laden and staggering when he returned to his car and he was glad to lay down his burden among the scattered items of fishing tackle in the boot.

He locked the boot, and left it locked when he reached home and garaged the car. Joan must not suspect that he had anything unusual in mind.

After supper, he spent the evening sitting quietly by the fire, which was his usual habit and therefore unremarkable. As soon as he decently could, he bade Joan 'good-night' and went to bed.

They had occupied separate rooms for so long now that Henry could barely remember any other arrangement. It suited him, because he preferred solitude, but tonight for perhaps the first time, he saw a real advantage in it.

In the privacy of his room, Henry packed a suitcase.

He chose the largest he could find and crammed it to overflowing with all the things he considered to be of practical use or value. To conserve space he kept spare clothing to a minimum, but he made sure to include plenty of handkerchieves and clean underwear. Toilet articles and towels were an important inclusion, as were half a dozen pairs of good socks.

He also took a few documents, in particular his cheque book and credit card, and a small sum of accumulated money.

Henry was not consciously aware why he did this, except that he had a purpose in mind. Whether it succeeded or failed, the purpose would leave him in a predicament. A creature used to comfort, he did not relish the prospect of spending many days unwashed, unchanged and penniless, but when he looked forward to what the future might bring he had to admit the risk that something like that might happen.

Hence the careful preparations.

He also had a strong premonition that in a few short hours, when he walked out of the house, he would not be returning.

Perhaps not ever.

★ ★ ★

Henry spent a short, uncomfortable night.

He didn't dare to sleep — doubted if he could have slept even had he dared — but even the risk would have to be avoided. He had decided to leave the house well before dawn, and that would mean a certain amount of creeping about in the small hours.

There was always the risk that Joan might wake, and since the entire escapade might be endangered if Joan came to hear of it, the use of an alarm clock was out of the question.

So Henry sat on his bed and played solitaire.

He played badly — inattentively — and whenever he felt drowsiness creeping on he opened the bedroom window wide and leaned out, breathing the night air.

By dint of will, he fought against sleep.

And by the time he had won that battle, it was time to leave.

21

TWO men with pint glasses — talking.

"You were supposed to be keeping nix, Basil," Frank Finch said in sulky tones. "Why didn't you whistle?"

Basil Jenks resented his companion's grumbling.

"How the hell could I?" he retorted. "We didn't expect the crafty sod to show up in the afternoon. Anyway, he was there in a flash, before I had time to do anything. You saw him as soon as I did."

"A fine bloody sentry you turned out to be," Finch sneered. "You hand me the dirty job to do and all you've got to bother about is watching. But you make a balls of that."

"Oh leave off, for Christ's sake," Jenks snapped. "I wish I knew what was biting you."

"You will if he goes to law," Finch said darkly.

Frank Finch was a worried man.

As a responsible member of Wiscliffe society, he could not afford to be involved in anything that smacked of scandal. There was no denying the enormity of what he had done, nor the fact that two people had caught him doing it.

Two people!

It wouldn't have mattered a damn if the man Crumblestone had been on his own, but having that piece of crumpet with him had balanced the odds in an uncomfortable way. And as if that were not enough, in his haste to leave Finch had left damaging evidence at the scene. Jenks had suggested that Crumblestone might not find the can, and that even if he did he was probably too stupid to recognise it for what it was. But Finch found that hard to accept.

And he couldn't accept Jenks' attitude, either.

Jenks was too bloody confident by half. He paid scant attention when Finch voiced his worries and he roundly pooh-poohed the idea that Crumblestone would bring any sort of action against them.

"Don't give Crumblestone another thought, Frank," Jenks said in jovial tones. "He's just a snivelling little rat, that man. No guts at all. He'll think twice and twice again before he has a go at you and me."

"He's got the goods on us this time, Basil."

"Rubbish! Stuff and bloody nonsense! I've got pull in this town, Frank, and there's no way Crumblestone can put one over on me. Two words out of place and we'll sue him for defamation. So leave off, man. Have another pint and forget about it. And if you must keep harping on, keep your bloody voice down. We don't want everybody to know."

So Frank Finch drank and tried vainly to forget, with the result that he became very much the worse for drink without showing much improvement in humour.

★ ★ ★

They were in the bar at the Wiscliffe Yachting Marina and Caravan Club. They had gone there early, fresh from the interrupted raid on Crumblestone's land, and even before the first regular patrons appeared, both men had taken a ration of drink.

As the evening wore on, more customers appeared and the main Club-room began to fill up. Drink flowed freely — as it usually did — but nowhere more freely than in the corner where Jenks and Finch stood supported by the bar counter. In spite of the oft-repeated warning from Basil Jenks, Finch continued to gripe and fret about the Crumblestone affair. Each pint of ale brought further freedom to his tongue, and since the other members knew nothing of the incident and would not have approved it if they had, Jenks was forced to work hard at keeping Finch silent.

The method he chose was to ply him with drink and overbear his conversation with tolerant shushing and loud apology for his condition before ordering still more drink. Inevitably, as midnight approached, Frank Finch was not only drunk, but drunken-ill.

When the time came for the bar to close, Finch's condition was serious and he had begun to alternate between maudlin volubility and unconsciousness.

Tom Ellis, a local butcher, was first to state the obvious.

"Frank can't possibly drive home, Basil."

"God, no!" Jenks agreed. "If he ever got as far as the main road he'd come to grief at the first lamp post."

"What's to be done, then? You going to ferry him home in your car?"

"Take Frank home with his tonsils floating? No fear! There'd be hell on if I did that. Frank's missus would have his guts and mine as well — and Frank'd never forgive me."

"For God's sake, then, what do we do with him?"

Jenks supplied a possible answer.

"He'd better kip down here, in the Club. Let the silly bugger sleep it off."

"What do you reckon his missus would say about that?" Ellis said, grinning.

"Buggered if I know, Tom. But that's his own business. He can sort that out when he's sobered up a bit."

But Peter Travis, who was the Club Secretary, sounded a contrary note.

"Sleep in the Club? That's not on, Basil. There's no bed or anything, and the chairs aren't suitable."

"He can doss down on the floor, Peter. He's too drunk to know the difference."

"He might be," Travis allowed, "but he's not stopping here. He's had a right gutful, and he'd sick it all up and stink the place out. Besides, we've got a

lot of pricey kit in this Club-house.
If Frank started roaming about in
his condition he could do a lot of
damage."

"All right then, you think of
something," Jenks snapped.

"Well, there's the office out back,"
Travis suggested.

"That bloody little caravan with the
broken window?"

"Yes. Why not? At least there's a
bunk bed in there. He'll sleep like a top.
And even if he doesn't, there's nothing
much he can spoil out yonder."

"He could freeze to death. I know
it's only October, but it can get bloody
cold in a van at this time of year."

"We can wrap him up. I've got
loads of blankets in the car, and all
those cushions in the office. He'll be
all right."

Jenks considered — then gave the
plan his approval.

"All right then, so let's get him in
there. Come on lads. You hold the
door, Peter. You grab his other arm,

Tom, and let's get the drunken little slob off to beddy bye-byes."

"What happens in the morning, when he wakes up?" Tom Ellis wanted to know. "Poor little bugger. He won't know if his backside's punched, bored or countersunk."

Wisely, Jenks thrust out the hand of comradeship.

"Leave that to me, Tom," he said. "I'll pop up here first thing in the morning and hustle him back home."

22

WHEN the moment came, Henry was wide awake.

He pulled up briefly at the entrance to Eden and sat in his car, casting a fond eye over the bowl of blackness that was his hallowed plot.

It wanted the best part of two hours to daylight, and these were the darkest hours if the old adage was to be believed. He had hoped for some assistance from the moon, but the sky overhead was dour and the ceiling of clouds hardly discernible.

The darkness was an obstacle, but finding his way about should be no great trick. And soon, there would be light enough. The Wissey was already visible as a few strips of distant glitter and Plattsford Bridge encroached on his vision in a great sweep of blackness as though it had been carved from jet.

It pleased Henry to see that his fence was still in place and his notice-board still stood in dominant silhouette. Given time, Jenks would change all that, but until he did, the impression of a well-maintained enclosure would continue to be presented to the world.

No time to moon about, though. There was work to be done.

He fired the engine and cruised the Rover into the lane which led northwards to the Wiscliffe Heron Angling Club.

A hundred yards later he steered into the lane's verge and parked. Then, laden with his fishing basket and the two carrier bags from the boot, he trudged back to the bridge.

There was more weight in the burden than he had imagined. The creaking basket-strap dragged at his shoulder and the basket thudded against his spine with every stride. The thin plastic handles of the carrier bags cut into his hands and stretched noticeably, threatening to give way.

No worry about witnesses at this time of morning.

Quite deliberately he climbed across the fence rather than unlock the gate and as soon as his feet scrubbed on the familiar path he found he could make easy progress. He had equipped himself with a hand-torch, but there would be no need to use it until he reached the jetty.

On his way through Eden he could make out very little detail about him, but there were squeaks and rustling sounds on all sides. Henry smiled to himself. The makers of noise were welcome friends — small wild creatures — the unseen life that shared Eden with him.

When he got to the jetty he used his torch to light the way into the punt and to stow his burden in the well. The creak of the mooring rope and the splash of disturbed water seemed much louder now than by day and he wondered how far the noise would travel. This was the first time he had handled any kind of boat in darkness and a punt was not the most manageable of small craft, but once his hands took their grip of the paddle he felt at ease.

Using an occasional gleam from the torch to guide him, he paddled the short distance from the jetty, around the protruding end of the chain-link fence and into the mouth of the Marina's channel. He tied up at the first available mooring and stepped ashore. He used the torch again whilst he transferred basket and carrier bags from the punt, and a stray beam picked up a glistening boat-like shape bobbing in the mouth of the channel. He focussed on the object.

A dead chub. Belly-up.

If Henry had been in need of a further spur to action the bloated white corpse supplied it. It was a cause for sadness but also for renewed anger. Henry, and men of his kind, preferred their fish alive and darting. To them, a dead fish was a tragedy, a butchered fish an abomination.

Henry moved off into the darkness and picked his way into the heart of the Marina. He was not completely lost. Years before, as a young man, he had attended a few dances and social functions there, which had given him some sketchy knowledge of the lie of the land. As far as he knew, it had changed little since then.

He found his way to the Club-house without difficulty and moved close alongside it, feeling the texture with his fingertips.

Wooden walls! Planks of dry and brittle timber!

The Club-house was a single-storey structure, built on cricket-pavilion lines, with a railed walkway along three of its sides. It was not a large building. At a careful guess it measured a hundred feet by eighty, the jutting walkways being additional to that.

It was time to begin, but first he listened carefully and his ears were rewarded with utter silence. He had expected nothing else. He knew the Club-house itself would be untenanted because there were no living-quarters attached, and no rooms suitable for adaptation. But Henry would have hated to be wrong, and as a precaution he checked all three doors. They were all double-leaf design, and all padlocked on the outside as he remembered them.

The inspection reassured him.

As for the caravans scattered about the compound, none of those were likely to be occupied. This was essentially a touring club and all the vans were tow-jobs. There would be neither ears to hear nor eyes to see. He had the entire establishment to himself.

Taking a packet from one of the carrier bags, he shone his torch on it. The light picked out a single word.

Firelighters!

Henry chuckled at the aptness of the name. Firelighters! He hoped they would do the job they had been designed for, because he intended to light a fire — and a big one.

To make sure it would be big, he had brought plenty of packets. Sixty packets in all. Eight hundred and forty individual white cubes. They represented the bulk of the stock of the hardware store and it was small wonder the shop assistant had seemed surprised. They hadn't come cheaply either. They'd cost him nearly ten pounds in total, but Henry still considered them a bargain.

There was nothing capricious or fanciful about Henry's choice of combustion agent. He had given the matter a great deal of thought, and although the various liquid fuels had seemed an attractive idea at first, he had discounted them finally. The Club-house, he remembered, like so many wooden buildings, was propped on short brick pillars and stood inches clear of the ground. Paraffin or petrol, he reasoned, might leak away too rapidly and evaporate harmlessly. Firelighters, on the other hand, were made specifically to burn *in situ* and they seemed a much sounder proposition.

Henry might have been right or he might have been wrong, but in the event his scheme worked well.

He made three consecutive circuits of the Club-house: the first to lay a row of firelighters at regular intervals along the base of its walls, jamming them into fissures where possible; the second to use up surplus cubes by packing them between those of the first row; the third to ignite them. The process took a long time and he used up five boxes of matches, but by the time he completed the third circuit, the entire Club-house was encased in a glowing ring of flames.

There was a small difficulty at the rear of the building, where a dilapidated four-berth caravan had been parked so close to the wooden wall of the Club-house that there was hardly enough space to squeeze through. Setting the firelighters between caravan and Club-house was a struggle, and applying a lighted match was doubly difficult, but he managed it.

When the Club-house was well alight, Henry stood on the cindery patch of hard-standing in front and watched the building burn. This, he remembered having read somewhere, was typical behaviour for the compulsive arsonist, and now he could see why. He was conscious of fierce elation and a profound sense of achievement. He felt righteously vindictive. He almost wished Jenks had been present, so that he could laugh in the other man's face.

And it also occurred to Henry that this was the first time in his life when he had ever seriously broken the law.

Surprisingly, he felt no twinges of conscience.

So much had been visited on him by those for whom this building stood that there was a basic rightness about his act of retribution. Henry had come in search of vengeance and he had found it. Illegal or not, his deed was amply justified.

He would have stayed to the end, to see the structure reduced to ashes, but at the height of the blaze he was disturbed by the frenzied barking of a dog. Moments later lights sprang on in the window of a caravan some distance from the Club-house and in the glow from the fire he saw shadowy human figures moving beside the lighted van.

It was time to be going.

He took the only suitable exit, along the main driveway and out through the main gates to the road. He moved fast, making no particular attempt to avoid being seen.

In the midst of flight, it occurred to him that he had left his fishing basket and the carrier bags behind and that they would probably point the hunt his way. Also, his punt still lay moored on Marina property where it would soon be found.

Ironically, the striking feature of Henry's punt was the brand new patch across the hole gouged into it by Jenks or Finch. They'd love that. Jenks and Finch would recognise that patch for what it was, and they'd delight in using it to deliver Henry into the hands of the police. He wondered whimsically if they'd bother to explain how the patch came to be there.

So there was evidence by the bucketful, but he was not unduly alarmed. In due course he was certain to be caught. 'Brought to justice' was the term the Press would probably use. But he wanted it to end that way. At heart, Henry had always intended that the world should know him as the culprit.

In particular, he wanted Jenks and Finch to know.

When they learned *who* — they would also know *why*.

But he wasn't quite ready to be caught yet.

Running like a hare, he passed the entrance to Eden, reached his car and drove away.

23

IT was a spectacular fire, but short-lived.

The combined effects of several hundred separate seats of ignition, evenly spread around the Club-house, led to a concentrated inferno, which ate up its available fuel rapidly and presently died from want of replenishment.

The old and tinder-dry timbers of the outer walls crackled and melted in the heat. The inner lining of painted hardboard blistered, curled and fell in smoking flakes. The roof joists grew weak and buckled and the heavier planks and tar-felt of the roof crashed in a blazing cascade, to consume furniture and internal fixtures in one glorious and savage burn.

The ramshackle four-berth caravan filled with smoke until, at the height of the blaze, its wooden frame and fittings caught fire.

Frank Finch died without waking.

The heap of blankets and cushions round his body glowed red and smouldered to powder. When the fibre in their make-up dissolved, the walls and roof of the caravan drooped and folded about the corpse and the whole pile pulsed with flame.

The fact of the fire was established early, but such was the speed of its progress that when the alarm was raised and the Fire Brigade appeared in answer to the urgent summons it was too late to save the building from complete destruction. The pumps chattered into action, but there was nothing left for them to do except suck water from the river and damp down the smoking pile of hot ashes.

But for once, there was no mystery about the cause.

Sub-officer Eric Murchie, the senior fireman present, suspected deliberate incendiarism from the start and used his expert knowledge to read the signs. Within a matter of minutes, he had discovered ample evidence to confirm his suspicions.

Added to which, there was talk of an intruder.

Young Mr and Mrs Steele, who were guests of a Club Member, had been staying temporarily on the site in their caravan. Towards morning, they had been awakened by the sound of their pet mongrel 'barking the roof off' and from their caravan they had seen the Club-house well alight. They had dressed and emerged to investigate. Mr Steele had seen nothing but the blaze, but his wife had noticed a figure — a male figure, she believed — running down the drive towards the main gates.

The police, in the shape of Police Constable Dan Ryan in his panda car, followed hard on the heels of the Fire Brigade, and Ryan's own prying yielded more facts, the sum of which caused him to summon expert help.

Detective Sergeant Jim Yates, freshly roused from his bed, sniffed about in the ashes and took possession of some interesting items, including a fishing-basket, some plastic carrier bags and a handful of spent matches which had survived the blaze. The sergeant interviewed the Steeles and took statements, including a sadly inadequate description of the suspect, as seen through the eyes of Mrs Steele.

Daylight surprised the toilers around the still glowing ashes, but by then the authorities had learned a great deal about the fire: the method used to start it; the nature of the combustibles; how and where they had been procured and how transported to the scene; the route taken by the fire-raiser in his approach and in which direction, after his work was done, he had made his escape.

They still did not have a motive — or a name to tag on the person responsible — and it fell to Basil Jenks to supply the missing details.

By an accident of timing, Jenks set out from home only minutes ahead of the policeman sent there to break the news. He came to the Marina by prior arrangement — to collect his drunken associate — and he knew nothing of the fire until he arrived. But, as Sergeant Yates and Sub-officer Murchie were to learn, Basil Jenks knew many things. He spoke to them — and they listened with keen attention.

Only then, did they discover the body of Frank Finch in the ashes of the burnt-out caravan. Only then could they circulate as '*wanted*' for Arson and for Manslaughter, one Henry Crumblestone.

And it was not until the evening of that day, when he bought an evening paper from a village shop some miles distant, that the same Henry Crumblestone learned the full truth — learned that his act of revenge had been more pointedly effective

than he could ever have imagined it
would be.

★ ★ ★

The news shocked Henry to numbness.

He felt no fear for his own safety,
because he had long since resigned
himself to the sting of retribution, but
he hated the thought of squandered
life and the revelation of Frank Finch's
demise appalled him.

A more vindictive man might have
seen the death as an unexpected profit
and been maliciously pleased about it,
but such feelings were not in Henry's
nature. Indeed, if it had been possible
to foresee this outcome, he would have
stayed his hand and the incident would
never have taken place.

Henry bitterly regretted being the
cause of another man's death, and
he deplored the cruel trick that
circumstances had played on him. That
the victim was Finch — and that Finch
had earlier wronged him — caused

Henry no satisfaction and brought him no solace. Indeed, had the dead man been Jenks, whom he regarded as his principle tormentor, he would have been no less dismayed.

But the deed was done, and nothing remained but the settling of the account, promptly and fully, in the coin of penitence. He would be arrested and he would be punished, just as he had foreseen from the start, and in punishment he would make amends.

In a perverse way, he was grateful for the chance to atone for his sins.

★ ★ ★

"Oh the fool. The stupid little fool."

Joan Crumblestone giggled and slid an elegant tongue into the mouth of her freshly emptied liqueur glass. "Look how it all sticks to the sides," she said, careless of syntax.

"Have another for God's sake," her companion said, and without waiting for her response he snapped his fingers at a passing waiter. "Another Tia Maria. And bring me a double brandy. Who's a fool?" he went on, conversationally. "I suppose you mean that bloody husband of yours."

"Yes. Simple little Henry. Can't you just see him there, running about and striking matches like a Boy-scout at a barbecue." Again she giggled, half-choked. "I'm not in the least surprised, you know. I've always said he was unstable."

Her companion grimaced.

"Unstable? That doesn't say the half of it. He must be a nut case. Stark staring bonkers. Nobody in his right mind does a stupid thing like that. Thousands of quids worth of damage for nothing, and a chap dead into the bargain. But take it from me, Joan. When they catch him, he's going to be bloody sorry."

"He'll get a long sentence, won't he?"

"A bloody long one, I hope."

"Poor Henry," she said, stifling another giggle.

★ ★ ★

They had dined expensively in a small but select restaurant well away from Wiscliffe, where they were frequent patrons. As usual, the service had been matchless, the cocktails deliciously dry, the consomme light and aromatic, the fish smooth textured and piquant, the steaks a tender heartbeat beyond rare and the wines full-bodied and strong.

"What do you suppose he'll do?" The man questioned as he sipped his second double-brandy.

"Do? Give himself up, I suppose. Frankly, I don't care what he does, as long as he keeps away from me. I'm never going to speak to him again. That's something you can absolutely take for granted."

He laughed coarsely — suggestively.

"Didn't speak to him much before this, did you?"

"Not much. The stupid little man. And not any more. I won't ever have him back. Not even if he comes crawling."

"You won't have to, Joan. The minute he shows up, he'll find himself cooling his backside in a cell. He'll be off your hands for years then, with any luck."

The smile left her face and her lips tightened.

"Oh no. Not for years. He'll be off my hands for ever."

"You'll definitely leave him, then?"

"Certainly. You surely don't suppose I could live with a criminal? The minute he's sentenced I'll petition for divorce. That's the only place where luck comes in. With any luck, I'll have the decree before he comes out."

"I don't think imprisonment's regarded as a valid ground," he said doubtfully.

"Nor do I." She laughed mirthlessly. "But there's always this latest thing, 'irretrievable breakdown of the marriage'. The way we've been for the past ten

275

years should be grounds enough. I've never had him near me."

"Is he likely to be dangerous?" the man asked. "To you, I mean."

"Don't be silly." She was giggling once more. "Henry daren't say 'boo' to me. If I ever see him again, I'll run him in myself."

They moved from table to bar and he ordered fresh drinks before continuing on the same theme.

"Well, he can't keep running for ever. Not with winter coming on. I'll give him a couple of days — no more."

"He's got the car, remember," she pointed out. But her companion laughed expansively.

"No he hasn't, Joan. Oh no he bloody hasn't. He'll have to ditch that, or he'll be picked up in no time. No, the car's the first thing he'll get rid of. And after that, he'll be restricted all round. How's he fixed for funds?"

"Money? He can't have much. He's taken his cheque book with him, though."

The man laughed again.

"Much good may that do him. He'll find that cashing cheques is a wee bit risky, what with his picture in the papers and all the coppers looking for him. Without ready cash he's on a hiding to nothing, is Henry. Unless he turns to crime," he added, grinning.

"You mean steal money?"

"Why not? There's plenty of it about. And don't try telling me your Henry's an honest man."

"Good Lord!" Her face became suddenly ashen.

"What's biting at you?" he said, puzzled.

"I've just remembered something," she told him. "If Henry thinks hard enough, he'll have no need to steal."

"You've lost me somewhere, Joan. I don't get it."

"No? Well you'll see in a minute, when I tell you that there's three hundred pounds in my wardrobe back at the house. It's what I've saved up. Henry knows it's there — and he's still

277

got his house-key, don't forget."

He savoured the tidings and frowned.

"Bloody hell! You've been careless, Joan."

"Haven't I just. I should have thought about that before. God! I hope I can get to it before Henry does. That's my money — all of it. I'd be sick if he got away with it — and him a murderer."

The man looked at his wrist-watch.

"Come on then," he said, "we're wasting time. Move out for Christ's sake. With a bit of hurry-up we can make it to your house inside half an hour."

* * *

Tyres drumming and headlights unwavering on full beam the metallic-silver Ford Granada thundered along the approach road to Wiscliffe at something like the ton.

It slowed as it entered the built-up area, but it still took the corner into

Waverley Crescent far too fast. Its nearside wheels lifted to the drag of centrifugal force and their treads lost traction. The car drifted towards its offside, out of control.

The woman screamed once.

Then, more noise, but not the sound of screaming.

24

AFTER the sound — silence.
The engine had stalled, but the headlights still blazed, floodlighting the scene. He climbed out and shook his head, aiming to clear the fuzzy, unreal sensation which threatened to bring up the contents of his stomach.

They'd claim it was the drink. Maybe it *was* the drink. But people were always talking a lot of poppycock about drink. They reckoned it dulled your senses and slowed down your reactions, but that was pure bunkum — and he'd just proved it.

Nobody could say he hadn't acted lightning fast.

He'd seen the tree appear in front of him and he'd reacted fast enough to catch pigeons. The small amount of damage proved it. He'd tupped the tree with his front bumper but he'd been nearly stopped by then and the only damage he'd collected was a bent bumper and a flake or two of paint chipped off the front offside wing.

The bumper would straighten, the dent in the wing would roll out, and a spot of touch-up colour would make the whole thing right as rain.

As for Joan . . .

Her body lay huddled at the roadside — a mad tangle of multi-coloured cloths, limbs and laces, sprawled in the gutter and harshly visible in the glare of the headlights.

He approached the bundle hesitantly. He couldn't see her face at all, because she was lying with her head doubled under her shoulders somehow. The one arm that protruded past the head was covered in blood and both her legs were twisted outwards, almost at right-angles to the body. Weighing it all up, Joan didn't look too healthy at all.

Climbing back into the car, he noticed the shiny white handbag lying in the front passenger foot-well. It was one he'd bought her quite recently — as a straightener after a little quarrel they'd had. She liked that handbag, and she'd want to have it with her. Besides, it wasn't the slightest bloody use to him.

He carried the handbag out of the car and placed it carefully on top of Joan's body.

There was the windscreen too, of course. Nothing left of that, except a few bits of powdery glass. He was wondering about the best place to get a new windscreen fitted as he drove the car away.

* * *

When Inspector Harry Shilton reached Waverley Crescent he was third in line and had to park his Vauxhall Viva Supervision-car behind a blue-and-white Ford Escort and a Yamaha Solo Motor-cycle.

Shilton was late duty Inspector covering Wiscliffe.

He had been out on patrol when the call went out directing any mobile to attend the scene of a 'failing-to-stop' in Waverley Crescent, and although the message had not been aimed primarily at him, he had picked it up and responded. He heard over the air that Panda Three with P.C. Sid Bucklee on board was attending, but Inspector Shilton was a conscientious supervisor and he wanted to make quite sure the incident was receiving the right sort of attention.

Bucklee met him as he climbed out of his car.

"What's in it, Sid?" Shilton asked.

"It's a fatal, sir. She's mutton all right."

"A woman, eh? Ambulance on its way?"

"Yes sir. Due along any minute."

Shilton walked along the crescent until he stood looking down at the body. Bucklee joined him.

"Have we found out who she is, Sid?"

"Provisionally, yes. Her name's Joan Westwell. She lives just a bit further along the street."

Shilton had been half listening. His eyes had picked up the figure of a man standing on the far side of the road.

"Who's the bloke over yonder?" he said suspiciously.

"He's all right, sir. Name's Harris. He rides the motorbike. He's the one who found the body and rang in."

"Has he made a statement?"

"Not yet. But he knows I want one, so that's all right."

There was a short silence before Shilton said:-

"You said 'provisionally' Sid. What was that supposed to mean?"

"Eh? Oh you mean the name. Well, her handbag's here. That's if it *is* hers. I've had a look through it and there's plenty of stuff inside — papers and letters. If the handbag belongs to her, then she's Joan Westwell. That's what I mean."

"Is there any doubt about it? Being hers, I mean."

"Not really doubt, sir. It's just a bit odd, that's all."

"Odd?"

"That's right, sir. When I first got here, the handbag was on the body. I mean *placed* on the body, just like it had been popped on a shelf. The body's all bashed about, as you can see, but there isn't a scratch on the handbag. Now why is it that whatever happened to *her*, didn't happen to *it*? I don't think she was carrying the handbag. I think somebody put it there *after* she was dead."

"Any witnesses?"

"Nary a one."

"So we can't explain the handbag yet. And we don't know what sort of car it was that hit her."

"It was a silver coloured job," Bucklee said. "Come and look at this, sir."

He walked past the body, stopped at the pavement edge and shone his torch on the ground. The beam picked up a cluster of uneven flakes, mainly dark coloured, but several of which were light and reflective.

"Metallic silver paint," Bucklee said. "The dark pieces are turned over, showing dark undercoat. I'll gather it up once we've got the body out of the way. And if you look over here, sir. See? There's a big lump of bark stripped off this tree. Something's given it a good old thump, and I'd say it was the car."

"So would I," Shilton agreed. "It looks as though the car hit the woman and the tree as well, more or less at the same time."

"That's what I think, sir," Bucklee said. "Except that I don't think the car exactly hit her."

"What do you think happened, Sid?"

"Well, just look at her hair, sir — and all round the inside of her collar. See those shiny dots? Bits of glass. Windscreen glass. And look at the way her coat's torn at the shoulders and each sleeve ripped away down the arms. That's drag damage for my money, and I don't mean dragging on the road."

"You trying to tell me something, Sid?" Shilton said.

"Yes. I think she took a header through the windscreen."

Shilton was not convinced.

"She hit the windscreen, certainly, but she can't have gone through it. If she'd done that, she wouldn't be lying outside on the road."

"Ah! But she would if she'd come *out* through it." Bucklee said. "I think she was a passenger in the car."

"And the driver drove away?"

"And the selfish bastard drove away."

★ ★ ★

The body had been shifted to the mortuary.

A description of the incident, with details of the suspect car, had been circulated to patrols. Inspector Shilton had returned to Wiscliffe Police Station, while Police Constable Bucklee was doing his best to find relatives and notify them of the woman's death.

Shilton was interested in the handbag.

He was checking the contents and listing the items for record purposes, and when he looked closely at the Driving Licence, he was perplexed. He had just sorted the little snag out when he heard Bucklee's voice coming over the radio.

"I can't rouse anybody at number nine," Bucklee grumbled, "and nobody round here seems to have heard of a Mrs Westwell."

Shilton grinned roguishly.

He had a high regard for Bucklee, who had proved himself to be an exceptionally gifted young man, but it would do no harm to take him down a friendly peg, and here was a glorious opportunity.

He grabbed the handset from a startled operator.

"You silly bugger, Sid," he shouted.

288

"If you'd read her licence properly, you'd have got her full name, instead of just half of it. It should be Crumblestone. Joan Westwell Crumblestone."

"Crumblestone?" Bucklee repeated questioningly. "Isn't that the name of the bloke they want for the fire at the Yachting Club?"

"Hell fire! Of course it is." Shilton said. "I thought I'd heard that bloody name somewhere before."

★ ★ ★

And so it was that the police — in the shape of Inspector Shilton — came to a totally erroneous conclusion, which for a few hours at least, threw their investigation into Joan Crumblestone's death a little out of line.

When Shilton checked the circulation put out earlier that day, naming Henry Crumblestone as wanted for fire-raising and the unlawful killing of Frank Finch, he noticed that Crumblestone was last known to be driving a dark blue Rover.

As he now believed, there was fairly convincing evidence that the wanted man had changed transport — a logical thing to do in the circumstances — and was currently driving something in metallic silver.

It had to be Crumblestone.

Who, after all, would be driving Joan Crumblestone home, except her husband? She was bound to have known that he was wanted by the police, but like many another loyal spouse she would have been ready to help him avoid capture. And who could blame her for that? They had had a secret meeting. Maybe it was she who had delivered the fresh car to him? And then, by a quirk of fate, she had herself fallen victim to his careless driving.

Shilton was pleased with his theory.

It explained why the driver had failed to stop at the scene. He had not been trying to avoid the consequences of the accident, he had been evading arrest for his earlier, more serious crimes. He had chosen to save his own skin at the possible expense of his wife's life.

The word 'possible' had its place in Shilton's theory because only a Doctor could ever be certain that a person was dead. The passing of Joan Crumblestone was now an established fact, but it could not have been so at the time of the accident. Crumblestone, for anything he had known, might have saved her, by obtaining medical attention at an early stage. Instead, he had taken flight.

That made him a selfish and heartless bastard in Harry Shilton's eyes.

Shilton caused an amended message to be circulated.

He changed no more than the description of the motor vehicle Crumblestone was now believed to be using, but he also cross-referenced the two incidents as being, potentially at least, attributable to the same man.

Henry Crumblestone would never realise the fact, but that circulation gave him some little respite.

25

THE moment he learned the news of Frank Finch's death, Henry set off to drive back to Wiscliffe and face the music.

With that aim in the forefront of his mind he kept to the main roads, making no attempt to avoid interception and capture. It was pitch dark by the time he reached Plattsford Bridge and although it would be impossible to see anything of the place he turned his car into the lay-by at Eden's entrance, doused the lights and climbed out of the car.

It was peaceful and relaxing just to stand there and smell the unseen river, even though the darkness hid all familiar detail from his eyes. It really was dark tonight, profoundly and abnormally dark. Much darker than it had ever seemed before, even though he had stood at this spot, at much the same hour, many times in the past.

What time was it, he wondered?

His wristlet watch had once been luminous, but age had dimmed it. He reached into the Rover and took a hand torch from the glove compartment. In the light of the torch, the watch showed ten minutes to nine.

He had never known the Wiscliffe Yachting Marina and Caravan Club to be swathed in darkness at this time. Always, before, there had been a yellow glow of light from that direction. Light and noise.

And then he had it.

No wonder the place was deserted tonight. There was no longer a place at which members could foregather. Henry himself had destroyed it. A Marina that could only be used in daylight hours? Now *there* was a curiosity. But it was so now — and it would be so for some time. Until a new Clubhouse was provided, the Marina would have to stay out of commission.

But it seemed somebody was still using the place.

The car, whose headlights he had seen approaching from the Wiscliffe direction seemed to be travelling slowly and a little erratically, and as it came to the entrance gates of the Marina it slowed even further, before swinging into the entrance and passing temporarily from his sight.

Henry was curious.

Whoever the driver was, he either lacked experience or had a full load of drink aboard. He had handled the car like a learner having his first lesson. Henry had nothing to do except wait to be arrested — and waiting could be a boring process — so why not satisfy his curiosity?

Keeping to the shadow of the hedge, he moved along the road and turned into the Marina. The red tail-lights of the car were still visible, well over to Henry's left and some fifty yards inland from the site of the defunct Club-house. Henry moved towards it, flitting between static caravans. As he approached, the car's lights went out, but there was still a little illumination and he realised that the driver, a shadowy moving figure, was holding a hand-torch while he played about with something.

Moving closer, Henry could make out the scene.

There was a long, low shed, built of corrugated metal sheets, similar to a school cycle shed. The car had been driven nose-first into the shed, but a large section of its rear end protruded. The figure holding the torch was in the act of draping a tarpaulin sheet over the exposed part of the car.

When the sheet was in place, the figure turned and moved away, passing within a few feet of the place where Henry stood in darkness. The torch was extinguished now, and Henry could make out no more than a silhouette as the figure passed him by.

But the silhouette was sufficient for recognition.

Basil Jenks!

It occurred to Henry that Jenks would hardly intend to walk home. He lived somewhere in Wiscliffe, and the nearest part of that town was getting on for four miles away. But then he remembered that there was a bus stop only a few hundred yards from the Marina's gate, and the service ran until ten o'clock at least.

To hell with Jenks, though. Henry was interested in the car.

Risking a few brief flashes from his own torch, he moved across to the shed and lifted the tarpaulin sheeting from the car. A Ford Granada, in metallic silver. Henry couldn't remember the registration number exactly, but he felt quite sure it was the same car.

Joan and Jenks?

Good God! What an unholy combination. And this charade of hiding the car — a charade which might have been happening for years as far as Henry knew — could only be their attempt to hide the truth from Henry.

As though he cared a jot! As though anything that Joan did, with Jenks or with anybody under the sun, would matter in the slightest to Henry.

But that theory wouldn't wash — would it?

Because they'd never really been discreet at all. He'd only *seen* the car once, parked outside his house, but it must have been there many times. Jenks must have driven Joan home times without number without giving a thought to whether Henry saw his car or not. So it made no sort of sense to think that this curious hiding of the car had anything to do with Joan or himself.

Jenks had hidden the car for some other reason.

What could that reason possibly be?

Henry was thoughtful as he made his way out of the Marina and back to his car. He had the feeling that he had stumbled onto some nefarious little matter in which Jenks was involved, but unless he did some further prying there was no way of discovering what it could be.

And Henry had no time to spare for prying.

Nor, to be quite honest, was he sufficient intrigued.

* * *

He drove sedately into Wiscliffe.

On the way, he passed two police cars and a uniformed policeman on foot, but they ignored him.

It might have seemed that the Devil was protecting Henry, in the accepted manner of that anti-deity, but the more mundane truth was that the police were looking for an entirely different car.

* * *

And because he reached Wiscliffe undetected, he made some minor changes in his plans.

To begin with, he was seized with the wish to make his peace with Mary

Dawkins and he could see no reason why he shouldn't stay at liberty long enough to see her.

She lived in a poky, one-roomed flat in a rambling old house on the edge of town, and Henry drove there by the shortest route. He approached without conscious care, leaving his car at the front gate, walking up the garden path and in by the front door, ringing the bell of her flat and standing in the lighted hall while he waited for her to come to the door.

Mary Dawkins was overcome, but once she had recovered from the initial shock and surprise she was glad to see him. She ushered him into the flat and asked no questions until the door had closed in his wake. Then she rounded on him, more in sorrow than in censure.

"Oh, Mr Crumblestone. Whatever have you done?"

What, indeed?

Well, it was very obvious that he had brought upset and grief to Mary

Dawkins. That much he had certainly done. He had also destroyed his own character, betrayed his upbringing and effectively put an end to all the basic freedoms he had been accustomed to enjoy. As the old Victorian Melodramatists would have put it, he had ruined his own life.

And he had also killed a man.

It was that last wickedness which troubled Henry most. The other things were serious too, but the death of Frank Finch overshadowed them all. It hardly mattered any more, that in committing those sins he had also gained full and fitting redress for the ills visited on him — on his beloved Eden.

"I'm truly sorry about Finch," he said with a wan smile. "I'd have preferred anything to happen rather than that. I never intended that anyone should die, Mary."

In the midst of sadness, she reacted to the word.

It was still 'Mary' evidently, as

though having used it once he had fallen into the habit. But it was a shame about the timing, a great pity it could not have happened in less troubled times. But his use of the name 'Mary' still endeared him to her.

"What will you do now?" she asked him.

"Do? Why nothing. Very soon they'll find me and take me away. I don't intend to make it difficult for them. I've never been one to dodge consequences, Mary."

She wanted to plead with him.

Quite deliberately — and in the face of a lifetime of moral integrity — she dismissed his guilt from her mind, discounted his crimes, found excuses for his culpability. She felt concerned for him beyond measure. Concerned and fiercely protective, as though just retribution were something she could fend away from him. In the stress of the moment she saw guilt as unimportant — his safety as paramount.

"You must deny it all, Mr Crumble-stone," she urged. "They won't be able to prove it was you."

Dear Mary. So reliable in support. But he shook his head.

"They can prove it all right. They've done that already, enough to name me in the papers. And it doesn't surprise me. I left so many things for them to find that a congenital idiot couldn't fail to work it out. But that doesn't matter a bit, Mary, because there's no question of me running away."

"But you can hide," she argued desperately. "Stay here with me, Mr Crumblestone. I'll hide you. I'll keep you safe. Nobody would ever think of looking for you here."

Again he shook his head.

"Stay out of this Mary, please! You mustn't become involved. I wouldn't have come here at all, except that I wanted you to know all about it. I knew you must have read everything in the papers, but you can never take what they print as gospel. I wanted you to hear it straight from me. I don't care about anything else, just as long as you understand and don't despise me."

She gazed at him, her eyes full of reproach.

"Despise you, Mr Crumblestone? Please don't talk like that. You know I could never despise you."

He nodded and smiled.

"Yes. I think I knew that before. But I'm certain now, so nothing else matters. I'll go now, Mary. But before I do, please listen to me carefully. The police are almost certain to come here. Even if I haven't been seen tonight, they'll check with everybody who knows me. So, sooner or later, they'll be here, asking questions."

"Don't worry, Mr Crumblestone. I won't tell them anything."

"Oh but you must, Mary. Don't make any attempt to cover up for me. In the end, I want to be found. So when they ask you, you must tell them exactly where to find me."

"But how will I know that? Where will I tell them to go?"

"There's only one place on earth, Mary," he said.

26

HE drove straight to where he wanted to be found.

It seemed fitting that he should return to Eden to spend the last of his freedom in that place. He parked the Rover in its usual spot, took his torch from the glove compartment and used it to light his way to the jetty.

An option faced him there. He could sit or stand. The wooden bench Sam Little and he had built offered more comfort, but he preferred to feel the ribbed timbers of the jetty beneath his feet and hear the waters of the Wissey lapping against the pillars on which the jetty stood.

He waited in silence, surrounded by almost total darkness, for almost two hours, and when the noise of dying engines warned him that the moment had come, he was too stiff and cold to move.

So he remained there, motionless, staring fixedly at the black, tarry surface of the Wissey. Over in the direction of the roadway there were lights and raised voices, the slamming of doors and the crunch of heavy feet on the paths of Eden. But Henry did not turn his head.

When the jetty shuddered thrice and a firm hand fell on his shoulder, Henry turned awkwardly on his heel and allowed them to lead him away.

★ ★ ★

Henry Crumblestone had been in custody for nearly two hours before he learned of the death of his wife.

Even then, Detective Sergeant Yates broke the news clumsily and grudgingly, seeming to take for granted not only that Henry knew already, but that it was Henry's doing.

Yates was in a *no-nonsense* mood.

He let the fact be obvious that his

primary concern was the fire at the Marina and the resultant death of Frank Finch, and it was plain that he expected a battle of words. He came to the interview with instructions from his superior officer, Detective Chief Inspector Paul Nichols, to soften Henry up and prepare the way for Nichols to come in later, with all guns firing, to blast a way through Henry's stubborn resistance.

As things turned out, Nichols and his figurative arsenal were superfluous, because a surprised Detective Sergeant Yates found his prisoner only too willing to tell all. Flustered by having stumbled into success, the sergeant made a hash of one official form and had to start again. Then, at Henry's dictation, he recorded a statement under caution, which amounted to a full and frank confession of guilt.

In two respects only, Henry was reticent.

He declined to say anything whatever about *why* he had committed the offences and he avoided all reference to his own occupation of land adjoining the Marina.

On the latter point, the sergeant was silent from sheer disinterest, and although he questioned Henry closely on the former, anxious to establish a motive, he conceded defeat after a few minutes of fruitless questioning.

And at that stage, Sergeant Yates introduced the matter which he believed to be routine, but which burst like a shell in Henry's ear and left him bewildered.

"Let's be knowing how you killed your wife."

Surprise, shock and utter confusion. The sergeant had spoken ill-advisedly and in ignorance. Henry dismissed the thought that he might be joking as soon as it arose, because nobody could be so sick as to use material like that. So three things — three very serious and unheralded items of news — were flung at Henry in the space of half a dozen words.

Joan was dead.

Somebody had killed her.

Henry was being blamed.

The sergeant's throwaway sentence had the force of a physical assault, and Henry shuddered. His '*What are you talking about?*' was a stunned verbal reaction with no conscious meaning behind it, but Yates misread the reply completely. To him it was no more than a clumsy attempt to stall. The prelude to a blatant lie.

"Don't give me that," he said bluntly. "You know bloody well what I'm talking about. And I've got news for you, Mr callous-bloody-Crumblestone. We've got reason to think she was still alive when you left her for dead. I'd think about that, if I were you, before I told any more flaming bloody lies."

The sergeant was angry, and in the heat of his passion he became coarse and unreasonable. Henry was filled with horror by the details leaking out from Yates' half-told story and he made futile efforts to discover the facts. In all innocence, he pleaded for confirmation of Joan's death, at the same time professing his own non-involvement. But Yates would have none of that.

"Where's the other car? How did you get rid of it?"

"What other car?"

More prevarication, Yates diagnosed. And it was all so bloody puzzling. Here was a bloke who'd been particularly open and honest about two very serious crimes, yet for some unknown reason he flatly denied a third. And in the third job, there was no evidence of 'intent' which, arguably, made it a less serious matter.

"Don't play games with me," he blustered. "You know bloody well which car I'm talking about."

"I assure you, I've no idea," Henry said huffily.

"The silver job. The one you had the bump in."

Mystified, Henry continued to refute the allegation.

"If by a 'bump' you mean a car

accident, I tell you quite frankly that I haven't had a car accident for . . . let me see . . . something like seven years. I collided with a bus on Miller Street. I was driving a Triumph Herald. A red one."

Henry spoke sincerely — and there is something about sincerity which has its effect on even the most disbelieving ear. The vibrations of truth in Henry's denials were reaching to Yates, but as yet, not strongly enough to completely convince him.

"Come on, don't let's muck about," he said. "You had a bump last night. No more than nine hours ago. In Waverley Crescent, close to where you live. You were driving a silver coloured car."

"Seven years ago," Henry said firmly. "And in Miller Street. Miles away from Waverley Crescent. I don't know what's on your mind, Sergeant, but I can assure you I've never owned or driven a silver coloured car, let alone had an accident in one."

"But you were with your wife. She was . . ."

"With Joan? You've got the story wrong somewhere, Sergeant. I haven't seen my wife at all for two days. We're not in the habit of riding in the same car. Anyway, you've just told me that my wife is dead. You didn't do it very kindly, but we'll let that pass. I know nothing at all about it, and I'm entitled to know. Don't you think perhaps it's time you told me what happened?"

It was Detective Chief Inspector Nichols who supplied the details. Yates suspended his stint by walking out of the interview-room and making a report to Nichols, convincing him that Henry Crumblestone was genuinely in ignorance of his wife's death. Nichols came in and spoke for some moments, tempering his words with compassion.

"And now, Mr Crumblestone," he said, when he had outlined the event. "I'm quite satisfied that you were not driving the car involved — and that means somebody else was. So I'd like you to help us if you can. I'd like you to think about your late wife's friends and associates. Do any of them own a car that's metallic silver in colour? Are any of them likely to have been driving in Waverley Crescent last night, with your wife as passenger? In other words, can you give us any information which would help us to find the man responsible?"

"I'm sorry, Inspector," Henry said, "but I've thought about that already, and I'm afraid I can't help. I've no idea who might have been with my wife — or who owns such a car."

And they believed him.

Because they were satisfied that Henry had answered truthfully in all other respects, Nichols and Yates accepted his single, blatant falsehood as the truth.

* * *

Later, in his cell, Henry spent a long time thinking about Joan, and wondering what effect her death would have on his own circumstances.

It would be wrong to say he felt no sorrow at the news, because he hated the finality of death, no matter whose house it visited. But it was impossible to feel the sort of personal sorrow he would have felt on losing a loved one, a person to whom he was deeply attached, a friend or even a close acquaintance.

Emotionally, he was not diminished by Joan's passing.

There would be a certain amount of upset when it came to settling her estate, but at least he had been able to persuade Joan, years before, to sign settlement papers. Mr Tomlinson, the senior partner in Henry's business firm, would take care of all that under the terms of an existing agreement.

And, financially at any rate, Henry would be better off.

Their joint assets would pass to him, and they were not inconsiderable. Moreover, if Henry's own private forecast of the result of his trial proved anywhere near the mark, he would not be able to waste those assets for some time to come. They would remain and appreciate. The house, he decided, would have to be sold. He would ask Mr Tomlinson to arrange that too.

It seemed shockingly improper to think thus, but Joan's death would bring him nothing but profit. And when he admitted that fact to himself it seemed all the more ironical that she should have been brought to death as a direct result of her cheating with that obnoxious fellow.

As for Jenks, Henry held a most telling card against the man. He had realised the card's strength as soon as the police passed on the story of how Joan had died.

Ought he to play that card?

There were two primary consid-erations. Firstly, he supposed, it was his duty to inform on Jenks in the interests of justice. Secondly, he owed it to himself to bring to book a man who had caused him so much pain and who also — as Henry had so recently found out — had been Joan's lover.

But there was no jealousy in him — neither was Henry a vindictive man. On careful reflection he lacked the will to bear witness against Jenks out of personal spite. And if he couldn't speak for that reason, why else should he speak?

He would say nothing of what he knew.

★ ★ ★

Basil Jenks was not at Joan's funeral.

Henry attended, travelling in a prison vehicle from the Remand Centre where he had been lodged to await the later stages of his trial. He was accompanied by two burly warders but, burly or not, they were kind, and on Henry's promise that he would not try to escape they spared him the indignity of wearing handcuffs.

316

But he was inadequately clad in rumpled pin-striped suit, and he felt ridiculous as he stood at her grave-side and paid lip service to convention. Nobody tried to communicate with him, and in the circumstances he was not surprised.

None of his own friends attended. Indeed, the mourners numbered less than a dozen.

And Jenks, he noticed, was not amongst them.

27

BUT Jenks was present at the Committal Proceedings which took place before the Wiscliffe Magistrates.

He seemed to enjoy every detail of the event, thundering his evidence from the witness-box and later, in the witness benches, sitting hunched forward on the edge of his seat and smirking broadly, like the old French Dames must have smirked when they knitted in the shadow of *Madame La Guillotine*.

Even at that early stage, Henry had already indicated through his Solicitor that he proposed to plead 'guilty' and to contest nothing. In consequence, the hearing was a short formality, the witnesses giving only the briefest of evidence and not being subjected to any cross-examination at all.

Jenks had let it be known that he wanted to say more, but the Court had restricted him to giving the bare facts. His pleasure at Henry's downfall showed all over his thick features, but he would have preferred to clinch the matter with observations of his own. Now, his deposition having been recorded, Jenks must be feeling the tiniest bit thwarted at not having been given the opportunity of ranting his hate in the sworn sanctuary of the witness box.

As only Henry knew, Jenks was doubly triumphant.

He had escaped the consequences of causing the death of Henry's wife by the simple expedient of running away, and now he had been present to play a part in Henry's own eclipse. Yet Henry had the means in his power to blunt the smug satisfaction Jenks must be feeling at this time. It would cause a most gratifying sensation in that solemn Courtroom if Henry gripped the Dock-rail and shouted:-

"*That man there. Basil Jenks. He killed my wife.*"

In his mind's eye, Henry could see the uproar such an outburst would have caused. He knew very well that he could never do it, but merely to think about it gave him some amusement. Henry was smiling overtly as the Chairman of the Bench, in sepulchral tones, announced his committal, in custody, to stand his trial at the next session of the Crown Court.

He was still smiling when they led him below.

★ ★ ★

Three days later, he was led from his cell at the Remand Centre to be confronted with a surprise visitor, Detective Chief Inspector Nichols.

Nichols was a decent sort. He had treated Henry with scrupulous fairness. Henry greeted him warmly.

"But why have you come to see me, Inspector?"

"Ah well," Nichols grinned. "We've had some success with our enquiries into the death of your wife, and I thought you'd like to know. In fact, we've interviewed a man and secured a confession. There are a few formalities to be gone through first, but I've little doubt we shall be charging him with causing your wife's death by Dangerous Driving."

So Jenks had fallen.

Nichols could only mean one man. It had to be Jenks. Henry's heart leapt wildly but he contrived to remain calm.

"I see," he said, hoping he sounded non-committal. "There's not a great deal I can do about it, but thank you for coming to tell me."

Nichols awarded him an old-fashioned look.

"I wondered if you might know the man?" he said, and he waited for a reply.

Henry sensed an underlying accusation in Nichols' words and in the way he uttered them. The man was toying with him.

"Know him . . . ?" he faltered.

"That's right. I just wondered. His name's Jenks. Basil Jenks. Funnily enough he's a big wheel at the Wiscliffe Yachting Marina. You know that place well enough, because that's where you had your little fling." His face darkened and he finished heavily, "Do you know him?"

"I . . . Yes. Vaguely."

"Vaguely, Mr Crumblestone? Are you sure it's only vaguely? Because frankly I've started wondering about you. You never did get round to telling us *why* you fired that place. Is it possible that I've stumbled on the reason?"

Not the real reason — but perhaps half the reason.

Nichols was plainly hinting that Henry had hated Jenks and that was the truth as far as it went. Nichols could not possibly know *why*, but he believed he did. He was seeing

Henry as a wronged husband who had avenged himself on his cuckolder. That was the wrong reason entirely — but it was a nice, tidy, acceptable reason and Henry thought he might adopt it.

"Does it really matter, Inspector?"

"Not really, but I think I'm right. I'd like to have it confirmed."

"Very well. Let's say I didn't like Jenks very much."

Nichols nodded and grinned.

"And now I'll bid you good-day, Mr Crumblestone."

He turned to leave, but Henry called him back.

"Inspector. A moment, please. Can I ask you how you found out it was Basil Jenks?"

"Oh! Didn't I tell you?"

Nichols walked back to the table, fumbling in his pocket as he walked. He flipped a visiting card on the table in front of Henry. It was one of Henry's own. There were letters and figures on it in Henry's scribble.

"We found that among your property," Nichols said. "It's a car registration number. Just out of curiosity we ran a print-out on the Police National Computer. Lo and behold, it's a silver Granada. And I think you know who owns it, Mr Crumblestone."

★ ★ ★

Many events — many surprises.

And all these things had happened to Henry Crumblestone in the course of a period which stretched like a lifetime into the past but in reality was only a few short months.

They had been hectic events. Henry remembered all of them and fitted each into its place in a majestic, sweeping tapestry seen in his mind's eye. The central figure of the whole picture was a gilt-and-white plaster cherub in the ceiling of Wiscliffe Crown Court.

The plaster cherub was fat and cuddlesomely humanoid, but one of its fingers — the little finger on the left hand — was chipped off at the first knuckle.

How could that possibly have happened? Henry wondered. The walls of the courtroom soared sheer, climbing twenty feet or thereabouts to reach the corner where the cherub hung and smiled. A flung stone might have reached it, or the carelessly wielded ladder of a painter or cleaning contractor. It seemed a shame . . .

The booming voice of His Honour Judge Deeping-Sproate was suddenly silent, and its ending was as startling as an outburst of sound. Henry jerked his head violently in the direction of the bench as he dragged himself back to the present.

"Eh? . . . What . . . ??" He stammered.

Mary Dawkins was looking hard at him. He could see her from the corner of his eye. And a little way over to Mary's right, Sam Little was watching him too. But the Judge had the strongest eye. Deeping-Sproate cornered Henry's look and returned it stonily before speaking again.

"The sentence of this Court," he repeated heavily, "is that you go to prison for five years."

28

IT is seldom desirable — or even possible — to know the future. Yet there is much human striving towards that end. Most people have wished for foresight from time to time and some have even claimed to possess it. No-one can be completely certain what fate has mapped out for him.

But a man who has just been committed to one of Her Majesty's Prisons for five years is more certain than most.

Henry's Counsel visited him in the Detention-area in the Court's basement, to wish him the best of a grim situation and to express regret that his advocacy had not produced a lighter sentence.

Henry knew very well that by his own refusal to contest the charges or to show due penitence he had made the

Barrister's task well nigh impossible. So he thanked the man heartily and assured him that his efforts on Henry's behalf had been entirely satisfactory.

After that, it should have been a short walk to the waiting Prison Van and a bumpy journey to a place of long term confinement, but it was obvious from a whispered conversation between his Warders that some other matter was in the offing.

Henry waited, faintly curious, and presently the Senior Warder approached him.

"There's an old bloke outside, asking to see you," the man said. "If you want to see him, we can let you have five minutes."

Sam Little! It had to be Sam.

"Yes please. I'd like to see him," Henry said.

And it proved to be Sam. There was an apprehensive look on his face, as though he doubted his welcome, but Henry was delighted to see him and, seeing it, he brightened.

"How's the head, Sam?" Henry said, grinning.

"Reeling. And I mean that. I didn't expect five years, Henry. Not with you being a first offender. I thought . . . "

"Let it be, Sam," Henry said sharply. "We've only got a few minutes, so don't waste it. Tell me about Eden."

"Funny you should say that, Henry. I've been doing a bit of work up there this last fortnight. I've had a bit of help from a friend of yours. A young lady."

"Mary Dawkins?"

"That's her name. She's quite a power-house, that girl. We've done some cleaning up, but we both reckon it's time Eden was left alone for the winter. So we've been getting things ready. We've shifted your boats — dragged 'em ashore and covered 'em with a canvas sheet. Don't worry about where the sheet came from. It's an old one I found in my shed."

"Thanks, Sam. That's good news."

"Maybe. But there's some bad news as well."

It was plain to see that the old man was trying to be serious. Henry stifled a jocular retort.

"What's that, Sam?" he said instead.

"Remember there was talk of putting a bridge through? Well it's going ahead. They reckon it'll be completed in a twelve-month, and they're starting any time."

A year, or not much more. In other words, the bridge would have become a thing in being long before Henry's sentence elapsed. Even allowed for full remission, he could expect to stay in prison for three years and four months — and by then there would be nothing left of Eden.

"That means the end, then, Sam."

"Yes, I'm afraid it does. And in a way it makes nonsense of what I've come to do."

He took a manila envelope from his inside jacket pocket and held it out to Henry.

"These chaps say you can have it," he explained. "It's a little gift from me, Henry. It's a poor gift in the circumstances, and to be quite honest I feel a bit of a heel for doing it this way. But I thought you'd like to have it, if only as a token."

Henry accepted the profferred package, whereupon Sam turned and trudged slowly away.

"Goodbye, Henry," he said. "I won't be able to visit you in prison, but I'll be looking forward to the day when you come out."

"Goodbye, Sam!"

It was a paltry parting word, but nothing else seemed in the least appropriate.

★ ★ ★

For a full minute after the old man had gone, Henry sat staring after him, only half aware of the package he clutched in his hand.

He had expected no gifts and wanted none, but when the brief trance ended he turned the envelope over and over

331

in his hands, assessing the contents. It bore neither printed detail nor written message, but it was fat and springy to the touch.

Using his thumb-nail, Henry slit the edge and drew the contents out. A wad of thick papers, neatly folded twice. With quickening awareness he opened the folds.

As a practising Solicitor, Henry had seen many such papers before, and to him the jumble of legal jargon was tolerably comprehensible. Phrases such as *'further assurance'* *'free from incumbrance'* and *'quiet enjoyment'* rolled glibly before his reading eye, but the portion which impressed itself most on Henry was in heavy print. It made reference to:-

' . . . *Samuel Mills Little, Gentleman, (hereinafter referred to as the donor) of the one part, and Henry V. Crumblestone, Gentleman (hereinafter referred to as the donee) of the other part . . .* '

He noted with wry amusement that the totally imaginary 'V' had become enshrined as fact, by inclusion in a legal document. This document was fully engrossed and absolutely valid. It was a deed of conveyance, and it described in detail a certain parcel of land which was unmistakable.

A poor gift, Sam had said.

But by the gift, Henry had become the lawful owner of Eden.

* * *

Less than a week later, Sam Little was dead.

Henry felt utterly devastated when he heard the news, particularly since Mary's letter arrived too late for him to put in a request to attend the funeral.

She had known it would be so.

" . . . I was there, Mr Crumblestone, because I knew you'd want me to be there," she said in her letter. "It was a lovely day, crisp and fresh. I bought a big bunch of flowers and put your name on them with a nice message. I know he liked you a lot, and he seemed a nice old gentleman . . . "

A *gentleman*. That was Sam Little.

For the first time in twenty years, Henry Crumblestone broke down and wept.

Sam had been a kindly man too, and a generous one.

According to the search-information and *evidence of good title* in the deed he had gifted to Henry, Sam Little had owned Eden for many years. Beyond doubt, he had owned the plot on that day some months earlier when, coming to view his own property, he had found it occupied by a meritless pretender, an interloper, a squatter.

Many a man — surely *every man* except Sam — would have answered Henry's intrusion with a battle-cry and a threat of legal action. But Sam had accepted it — even *condoned* it. For some inexplicable reason of his own, Sam Little had *wanted* Henry to possess Eden — and there could be no more convincing evidence of that, than his final gift.

Learning for the first time the calibre of the man whose rights he had usurped, Henry felt bitterly ashamed of himself. And his sense of shame was not relieved when he remembered that Sam had responded to his impertinence by seeking to become a guest on his own property.

'I didn't think you'd mind if I had a little walk around.'

Looked at in retrospect, the sentence was both humble and proud, laughable and sad, wise and ludicrous and utterly, utterly generous.

★ ★ ★

More than ever now, Henry felt the need to hang on to the little triangle of land, even though he recognised that its days of undisturbed peace were numbered.

When Mr Milner, of the Legal Department at County Hall, came to see him as new legal owner of the property to discuss the terms for compulsory purchase. Henry knew he would have to bow to bureaucracy in the end. But he had known Milner professionally for many years and he felt entitled to seek some answers.

"How much will they pay me, Tom?"

"Not a lot, I'm afraid. It's such a small plot, you see. No buildings on it, unless you count that broken down old shanty, and you can take it from me, Henry, they won't count that. The County will buy it in as undeveloped land with low rateable value, and they won't pay out much for that."

"And suppose they don't use it?"

"I'm not quite with you, Henry."

"Well, I mean suppose they don't build the bridge after all?"

"They'll build it all right. Don't you worry about that."

"I don't want you to fob me off, Tom. I said suppose they don't. Just *suppose*. Would they give me back the

336

land, on repayment?"

Milner pulled a face.

"The position won't arise, Henry," he said. "The contracts are out already. It's only a question of time."

"You're dodging the issue, Tom," Henry said sternly. "I know there's no chance they'll drop the project, but I still want to know what would happen if they did. Would I get the land back?"

"Offhand, if you want to be hypothetical, I should think you would. There was a time when Government Departments were a big naughty in that area. They used to acquire land on compulsory purchase and then sell it off at a fat profit when they found they didn't need it. But then they burned their fingers over some land at Crichel Down in Dorset, and that set them back a bit. After the Crichel Down affair, I should think you could recover without much trouble. But don't bank on it, Henry. This land will be used. We're definitely going to build a bridge."

"And I suppose I'm bound to sell you the land?"

"You've no option, once the Order's made."

"Can't I just give it to you — with conditions?"

"What sort of conditions, Henry?"

"Oh, nothing very restrictive. Just a sort of saver for if there is a change of heart. Let's say an agreed clause that if they don't use the land to build a bridge, it reverts to me."

"With a time limit, you mean? A sort of penalty clause?"

"Lord, no. Just a straight reversion. As long as they don't use the land, I can use it."

"I might sell them a scheme like that, Henry," Milner said thoughtfully. "But they'd want an unfettered right to build at any time — and they'd want it in writing."

"They can have all that, Tom. Just as long as they leave the title with me."

29

THE little compromise pleased Henry immensely.

It was a way of hanging on to Eden until the bitter end. Even though he could not enjoy it now, and even though it would have gone out of existence before he ever returned to it, he *owned* it.

He could always remember it as it was.

And the comforting knowledge that he was the rightful owner of Eden was an inspiration to Henry, sustaining him through the long years of his confinement. Eden, and other memories — other realities.

From the first closing of the prison gates he accepted as stark reality the fact that he would be a prisoner for a minimum of two thirds of his total sentence. Assuming he behaved himself — and Henry had no intention of committing even the tiniest indiscretion — his term of captivity would be three years and four months. He knew the figures off by heart. He had made the calculation many times.

Mary Dawkins visited him regularly. Her visits were too short and too impersonal. They could see each other clearly, yet they were separated by a screen of toughened glass strips, and the position was not helped by the knowledge that similar meetings were taking place simultaneously at adjoining tables. But it pleased and reassured him to know that Mary was prepared to travel a distance of eighty miles (one hundred and sixty miles in the round trip) just to spend a cramped and brief period in his vicinity.

In spite of their serious limitations, Henry enjoyed Mary's visits beyond measure. The chance to speak to her — about anything whatsoever — was reward enough, but she also brought him news about Wiscliffe and events there.

It was Mary who told him about the outcome of the trial of Basil Jenks. She was deeply disgusted by it. A fine of five-hundred pounds and a disqualification from driving seemed a puny sentence against Henry's five years. And there had been a death in both cases. Mary was very bitter about it, until Henry explained that Joan's death had been unintentional on Jenks' part.

"So was Finch's death on yours," she grumbled.

"Ah yes. But the fire wasn't. Don't you see, Mary, I burned that building quite deliberately — with intent, as they say — and that made Finch's death more blameworthy in the eyes of the law."

But much more importantly, she brought him news of Eden.

Since Sam Little's death she had taken to visiting the plot regularly. She was its only visitor. Since the poisoning incident which had led to such serious consequences there had not been a stick of damage done, and the news pleased him.

She was able to describe the changes of the seasons for his besotted enjoyment. She told him how she tended the flowers, weeded his paths, sorted his tools and fittings in The Fortress and kept the building clean, how she painted his fence, varnished his notice-board and pruned his shrubs and bushes.

Henry listened through a composite total of many hours of such description. He loved every word of it. He found it intensely comforting to know that during his enforced absence, Eden had a devoted custodian in Mary Dawkins.

★ ★ ★

Inevitably she brought news of the new bridge.

For long months, the project had not been mentioned locally, but when details began to appear in local newspapers it became quite obvious that the bridge-work was under way.

Mary brought him current reports of public meetings, announcements, artists' impressions of the finished bridge, plans of proposed routes and a wealth of other information, all gleaned from press-coverage.

And when the actual excavations and building work commenced, she went regularly to Eden to see the various stages for herself. Afterwards, she described them in detail to Henry, listing each new outrage in bitter terms. At first he shared her dismay, but after a while he became reconciled to the situation and was able to discuss it philosophically.

Much later, when the bridge was a reality and in regular use, she went again to look and learn. When she came to describe the visit to Henry she was deeply despondent, but he would not share her mood.

"They have every right to hack the land about, Mary," he told her. "I've given them that right. And when you think about it, the thing they've made is for the good of the whole district. It's for everybody, including you and me."

"But they've ruined Eden," she wailed.

"Don't worry about that. Some day, when I'm out of this place, we'll be able to drive across that bridge, Mary, and it will have special memories for us. Memories that nobody else can possibly have. Because we'll know it stands on a bit of earth that used to be ours."

"Ours? Mr Crumblestone."

"Yes, ours. After all the work you've done there, and all the help you've given to me, Mary, it could hardly be anything else."

"Some day," she said wistfully. "But when will that day be, Mr Crumblestone?"

"Not as long as you think, Mary," he said brightly. "The months have skipped by and there aren't many left. I should be out of here in a little under seven months."

He was released in May, and it was a cold, cold May.

Quite intentionally, and as a matter of policy, he had kept the precise date a secret. If Mary had known, she would have been there to meet him, ready to offer help and friendship. And the fuss, even a happy fuss such as that would have been, was the last thing Henry wanted.

Before he even began to make a new life, Henry had a long standing mission to perform. Freshly released, he was off to see at first hand, exactly what they had done to Eden.

★ ★ ★

He travelled to Wiscliffe by train, arriving there in the early afternoon and stepping onto the streets of that well-remembered town like a returned prodigal. They were wet streets. The bloom of May might be showing on the hedgerows, but the unhappy sky wept thinly and copiously.

Henry made his way to the bus station and boarded a bus destined for Plattsford. He booked to the fare-stage on the far side of Plattsford Bridge, because that was the nearest stop to the bridge itself.

It was rather like a school outing remembered from childhood, except that he was lonely in a crowded bus. The faces around him were not familiar faces, and although people chatted and smiled to each other, Henry was not part of their company.

For a while, he glanced around surreptitiously at his fellow passengers, enjoying the feeling of being free to go wherever — do whatever — he chose. No need any longer to obey petty rules or acknowledge irksome disciplines. Merely to exchange looks with people, innocently and without commitment, was a sweeping freedom in itself.

But before long he grew embarrassed,

conscious that he had been staring. He became acutely aware of his own white, unhealthy face and his damp and wrinkled suit. People would be bound to know him for what he was. The magic of the moment evaporated. Henry huddled down in his seat and looked pointedly out of the window.

He was still looking out of the window when the bus pulled in at the stop before Plattsford Bridge, and quite by chance his eye fell on a notice board in the front garden of a detached house.

It was a well-painted notice. A craftsman-made job. A notice that would last. In some ways it was not unlike the notice he'd made and painted himself, nearly four years earlier. The size was about the same, the wood of similar quality and the workmanship well up to Henry's own careful standards.

The words were entirely different, of course.

His own notice had borne his name

and address and some nonsense about 'Private Fishing' and 'Trespassers' being prosecuted, whereas this one had clearly been put up by old Thorneycroft, the Estate Agent, and all it said, in outsize lettering, was 'For Sale.'

The bus had moved off and was beginning to gather speed when the impulse to stay and admire the notice came to him.

It was an irresistible impulse.

Henry climbed to his feet, swung on the passenger rail at the entrance and hurled himself out to the roadside, stumbling to his knees before he could recover his balance. He heard raised voices assaulting him from within the vehicle, but he shrugged them off.

It really was an excellent notice.

In addition to the larger words, details of Thorneycroft and Company were shown in smaller lettering. Henry looked at the house. It was a nice house — not too big — well kept and with a good piece of garden front and rear.

There were no curtains at the windows and the rooms were bare. They'd soon sell that one, he reckoned, and with a notice-board as good as the one they'd used, they deserved to make a profit.

★ ★ ★

Henry was cheerful on the last leg of his journey.

It was still a good half-mile to Plattsford Bridge, but he stepped out jauntily, enjoying the exercise.

And, long before he came to Eden, he saw the new bridge structure ahead of him.

It was solid, brown and handsome. A beauty of a bridge. If something had had to be built there, Henry could have asked for nothing better. He moved towards it. With five hundred yards to go, his feet pounded on new tarmacadam.

The beginnings of a dual-carriageway.

30

EVERYTHING had changed.
Everything was brand spanking new. But if there was anything left of the old, Henry intended to find it.

Timidly, scarcely daring to put one foot in front of the other, he advanced towards the river, looking about him as he went. The first sight to meet his eyes was the Club-house of the Wiscliffe Yachting Marina and Caravan Club, a Club-house as new as the bridge — as new as the dual-carriageway.

It was a handsome building in red brick, with a properly slated roof and concrete steps leading up to an impressive front entrance. The building was only slightly bigger than the old Club-house, but obviously much much better.

Henry smiled to himself, remembering.

In a manner of speaking, they owed their new building to him. In that one sense he was the Marina's benefactor. But then he remembered Frank Finch and was at once disgusted by his own sick humour. The smile faded.

He was puzzled to see that they had built the new Club-house a lot nearer to the road, when it would have been much more logical to use the original site, much nearer to the river. He looked for the old site — and it was missing. He found the river bank and moved his gaze inwards, and that gave him the answer.

They had used the old site. The new building stood in exactly the same position as its predecessor in relation to the River Wissey.

The road had moved.

It was quite true. The new section of road was a continuation of the new bridge and it took a wide sweep in the direction of Wiscliffe, slicing off at least half of the Marina's territory. Henry had already half-noticed that there were far fewer caravans parked in the compound than had used to be the case. And no wonder! There simply wasn't room for any more.

Basil Jenks wouldn't think much of that.

It was strange that he should think of Basil Jenks after such a long time, when he thought he'd managed to eliminate the man from his system. But thinking about Jenks had reminded him of the chain-link fence and his eyes swept over to the right of the new Club-house.

The fence was still there — or part of it was.

The last few sections of the fence still marched down to the river's edge as he remembered it, identifying the precise spot where Jenks had first accosted him, all those years before. But now, far from being a majestic and gleaming barrier, the fence looked pathetic. It hung in stretched loops and most of its barbed-wire topping was gone. No more than ten yards back from the river's edge, the fence merged with the embankment of the new bridge in a tangle of rusty, clay-encrusted wire.

Yet it was not the fence that held Henry's attention so much as the landmark it gave him. Somewhere — only a few feet upstream of that fence — lay Lake Ceylon as he remembered it. Plain to see, the pool was no longer there. Quite literally it had been obliterated, steam-rollered out of existence, to make way for a mass of man-built earth and masonry almost as big as the pyramids of old.

Until that moment, Henry had come to terms with his loss of Eden, but the realisation that Lake Ceylon had completely disappeared from the face of the earth left him shocked and miserable. He turned away from the sight and wandered off, completely oblivious of where he went.

Unguided, his feet led him across the new section of roadway in a northerly direction. He passed almost under the wheels of passing vehicles and car-horns blared their disapproval, but Henry was so utterly disheartened by then that he would not lift his head. He came to a strip of rough land bordering the new road, crossed it and found himself looking directly at the original Plattsford Bridge.

The bridge was still in use, but now it was the second leg of the dual carriageway and would only carry southbound traffic. Nevertheless, the stones were the same, and in appearance the structure had not changed. It was the bridge that had once bordered his favourite piece of land.

Henry began to look for other familiar things, tracing a pattern from memory of what the place had once been like. It was then that he realised precisely where he was standing. Before him, lying at his feet with only a short vertical embankment intervening, was the gateway where his fence had formerly stood. Looking outwards from this point towards the river, he beheld what was left of Eden.

At any rate, there was still something left.

The two bridges stood parallel, but not close together. Far away on the opposite bank of the Wissey they separated like a forked tree branch and swept to left and right of him before merging again, somewhere to his rear. Between the two bridges an elongated egg remained, which was part-river and part-land. In a sense, Eden still remained, though it was less than half the size it had once been.

And what a dreadful mess it was.

There was mud and clay everywhere. Not a bush or a plant remained where his garden-beds had once been — not even a healthy blade of grass. Towards the river, where once a great reed-bed had blown, there was just a wide expanse of churned clay and yellow shale. Imported material, Henry presumed. Infilling spoil from excavations elsewhere.

The river bank still had a few of its willows, but they were poor, scraggy things, their leaves encrusted with clay-dust and their branches sagging. Between the sparse willows the river-bank was bare and brown.

The Fortress was still standing.

It appeared to Henry that its shell was undamaged, but there was no glass in the two visible windows and the door — or what remained of it — hung at a crazy angle.

And yet, in that corner, beside and beyond The Fortress, the havoc seemed decidedly less pronounced. Right against the old bridge, where the first span began its flight across the river, he could see the clumps of elders where he had once hidden to catch Basil Jenks and the late Frank Finch at their despicable tricks. Those elders, at least, seemed none too badly scarred.

In fact, the whole upper corner of the plot seemed greener, more alive than the rest, though it was a pitifully small part of what had once been Eden. And yet, there was still plenty of access to the Wissey here. At a rough guess, he reckoned there must be twenty yards of river bank, clothed with reed and willow and perhaps fifteen yards more, downstream of that, composed of horrid clay.

But there might be possibilities still.

He reminded himself that, such as the remnant was, he was legal owner of it. In the terms of the agreement he had with the County Council, since they had not used the whole of it, the residue remained with him. It might be no bad idea to survey what they had left him.

Stepping from the new road, he advanced into a sadly shrunken Eden. He picked his way through rut and puddle until he came to the threshold of The Fortress. Inside was a riotous mess. Most of his tools and equipment seemed to be missing and the few that remained were scattered about and lay rusting. In one corner, a heap of broken bottles and other rubbish was an obvious relic of occupation by the construction workers.

He came outside and passed behind the building and when he first saw the long, canvas-covered mound he was nonplussed. But then he remembered. Both Sam and Mary had spoken of his boats and how they had covered them. He lifted a corner of the canvas and peeped under. They were still there. And by the look of it, they were still in reasonable condition. A bit of a clean up and they would be usable — if he had a place to launch them.

His jetty had gone completely. But wait a minute . . .

No. The jetty was still there. He could see the upstream timbers of it, protruding from behind a heap of tipped rubble. He worked his way down to the spot, to make quite sure, only to find that he had been half right. The far end of the jetty, where it had overlooked Lake Ceylon, was completely gone, replaced by rough yellow artificial shoring.

But a dozen planks at the upstream end of the jetty were still in place and, by the feel of it, still firmly anchored to their supports. And upstream of the jetty there was still a good thirty yards of ravaged river bank.

It was river bank, though, and it gave access to the Wissey. If he extended the jetty a little, dug over the strip that now lay like an island between the two bridges, levelled out the humps of rubble, shifted the brickbats, imported some better soil, laid a path or two, planted fresh shrubs and flowers: if he did all those things and more, wouldn't he be left with another, much smaller but still desirable Eden?

No! Very sadly, he would not.

Because Lake Ceylon had been the centre of the old Eden, its focal point and its founding feature. And Lake Ceylon was gone.

The mad moments of misplaced

enthusiasm were over, and Henry allowed dejection to fill the vacuum of their going. Without that little secret pool, the place was less than a shadow of itself.

He remembered the spring that had once existed, rising from the ground to trickle riverwards and feed the old Lake Ceylon. Spring and pool were both hidden now, beneath tons and tons of earth. And yet, could they simply build-over a natural spring? He doubted it, and doubting made him wonder how the engineers had solved that problem. Rising to his feet he crossed over towards the new bridge, to have a look.

They hadn't eliminated the spring. They'd simply altered its course by piping it from the bridge foundations. Its waters now emerged from a nine-inch pipe in a steady, shining flow, and trickled their way alongside the bridge, *en route* to the river.

Henry followed the course of the little stream with renewed interest, rounding a pile of tipped rubble along the way. Ten yards short of the river, the stream cascaded into a pool.

It was not a large pool, but give or take a foot it was as large as Lake Ceylon had been. And it was deep, certainly. The water seemed clear enough, but he could see no sign of the bottom. The pool tailed off to a narrow channel beside the leading arch of the bridge, but the channel continued onwards to join the main river.

There was good access. If any fish were interested they could get in.

But compared with its predecessor, the pool was a sorry, naked thing. There were a few rushes at its tail, but at its head, nothing but bare bank. The little stream welling from the spring ran into the pool along a trough of barren yellow clay.

Encouragement? Discouragement? The pool offered neither — nothing.

Henry went back to his boats

and completely uncovered them. They looked good and solid. And somehow, looking at them, he began to hope again. There really was no reason why he should not launch them here. He could build a new jetty, cut a new launching-ramp. No doubt about it, if he tried really hard he could be back in business come the summer, with a new entrance, a new notice-board, a completely new landscaping job. It would be a damned hard slog — far harder than the first time — but it would surely be worth-while in the end.

And this time, he could ask Mary to help him.

If only Lake Ceylon had still been there, instead of that newly formed rough basin of clay. Was it possible, he wondered, to plant fresh reeds there, to make plants grow and in the fullness of time to persuade good chub to return and make their home in the new pool? He doubted it very much — doubted it so much, in fact, that he was not conscious of the will to try.

He grasped the canvas sheet and began to roll it back into position over the two boats. He had almost completed the task when something clinging to the underside of the sheet caught his eye. He identified it and grinned appreciatively.

A fat, black slug.

Beautiful creature. He picked it up, weighed it in his palm and thought back to other days. If there should have happened to be an old chub about . . .

He turned and made another crossing towards the new bridge, stealthily this time, slowly and on tip-toe. The very instant he came within sight of the new pool he stopped, gauged the distance and tossed the slug.

A perfect flight, judged to a nicety. The slug dropped into the centre of the pool with a plop.

Not just a plop, but a swirl. A mighty swirl.

Henry saw no more than that, but it was plenty. It was as though he had touched a button that concentrated his feelings, so that all the things he felt, hoped and planned for came together at once.

He twisted and began to run.

★ ★ ★

Running as he had never run before, Henry tore out of Eden and along the old road, heading for Wiscliffe. By the time he came to the bus stop he was thoroughly out of breath, but he stopped at the 'For Sale' notice and memorised the telephone number and the pause restored him.

Saying the number over and over in his mind, he began to run again, and two hundred yards beyond the stop he came to the telephone kiosk he had known was there. He recovered his breath as he fumbled for coins.

He rang the number, spoke to Thorneycroft and Company and made them an offer they could not refuse.

Then he took a triangle of yellow paper from his wallet inserted more coins and dialled the number on the paper.

He rehearsed his little speech while he waited for the call to go through, and when the moment came he said it without a falter.

"Mary? This is Henry! Will you marry me?"

The split second until she gave her answer seemed to hang like a lowering cloud — but suddenly, everything was well.

"You know I will, Mr Crumblestone," she said.

THE END

Other titles in the Linford Mystery Library:

A GENTEEL LITTLE MURDER
Philip Daniels

Gilbert had a long-cherished plan to murder his wife. When the polished Edward entered the scene Gilbert's attitude was suddenly changed.

DEATH AT THE WEDDING
Madelaine Duke

Dr. Norah North's search for a killer takes her from a wedding to a private hospital.

MURDER FIRST CLASS
Ron Ellis

Will Detective Chief Inspector Glass find the Post Office robbers before the Executioner gets to them?

A FOOT IN THE GRAVE
Bruce Marshall

About to be imprisoned and tortured in Buenos Aires, John Smith escapes, only to become involved in an aeroplane hijacking.

DEAD TROUBLE
Martin Carroll

Trespassing brought Jennifer Denning more than she bargained for. She was totally unprepared for the violence which was to lie in her path.

HOURS TO KILL
Ursula Curtiss

Margaret went to New Mexico to look after her sick sister's rented house and felt a sharp edge of fear when the absent landlady arrived.

THE DEATH OF ABBE DIDIER
Richard Grayson

Inspector Gautier of the Sûreté investigates three crimes which are strangely connected.

NIGHTMARE TIME
Hugh Pentecost

Have the missing major and his wife met with foul play somewhere in the Beaumont Hotel, or is their disappearance a carefully planned step in an act of treason?

BLOOD WILL OUT
Margaret Carr

Why was the manor house so oddly familiar to Elinor Howard? Who would have guessed that a Sunday School outing could lead to murder?

THE DRACULA MURDERS
Philip Daniels

The Horror Ball was interrupted by a spectral figure who warned the merrymakers they were tampering with the unknown.

THE LADIES
OF LAMBTON GREEN
Liza Shepherd

Why did murdered Robin Colquhoun's picture pose such a threat to the ladies of Lambton Green?

CARNABY
AND THE GAOLBREAKERS
Peter N. Walker

Detective Sergeant James Aloysius Carnaby-King is sent to prison as bait. When he joins in an escape he is thrown headfirst into a vicious murder hunt.

MUD IN HIS EYE
Gerald Hammond

The harbourmaster's body is found mangled beneath Major Smyle's yacht. What is the sinister significance of the illicit oysters?

THE SCAVENGERS
Bill Knox

Among the masses of struggling fish in the *Tecta*'s nets was a larger, darker, ominously motionless form . . . the body of a skin diver.

DEATH IN ARCADY
Stella Phillips

Detective Inspector Matthew Furnival works unofficially with the local police when a brutal murder takes place in a caravan camp.

STORM CENTRE
Douglas Clark

Detective Chief Superintendent Masters, temporarily lecturing in a police staff college, finds there's more to the job than a few weeks relaxation in a rural setting.

THE MANUSCRIPT MURDERS
Roy Harley Lewis

Antiquarian bookseller Matthew Coll, acquires a rare 16th century manuscript. But when the Dutch professor who had discovered the journal is murdered, Coll begins to doubt its authenticity.

SHARENDEL
Margaret Carr

Ruth didn't want all that money. And she didn't want Aunt Cass to die. But at Sharendel things looked different. She began to wonder if she had a split personality.

MURDER TO BURN
Laurie Mantell

Sergeants Steven Arrow and Lance Brendon, of the New Zealand police force, come upon a woman's body in the water. When the dead woman is identified they begin to realise that they are investigating a complex fraud.

YOU CAN HELP ME
Maisie Birmingham

Whilst running the Citizens' Advice Bureau, Kate Weatherley is attacked with no apparent motive. Then the body of one of her clients is found in her room.

DAGGERS DRAWN
Margaret Carr

Stacey Manston was the kind of girl who could take most things in her stride, but three murders were something different . . .

THE MONTMARTRE MURDERS
Richard Grayson

Inspector Gautier of Sûreté investigates the disappearance of artist Théo, the heir to a fortune.

GRIZZLY TRAIL
Gwen Moffat

Miss Pink, alone in the Rockies, helps in a search for missing hikers, solves two cruel murders and has the most terrifying experience of her life when she meets a grizzly bear!

BLINDMAN'S BLUFF
Margaret Carr

Kate Deverill had considered suicide. It was one way out — and preferable to being murdered.

BEGOTTEN MURDER
Martin Carroll

When Susan Phillips joined her aunt on a voyage of 12,000 miles from her home in Melbourne, she little knew their arrival would germinate the seeds of murder planted long ago.

WHO'S THE TARGET?
Margaret Carr

Three people whom Abby could identify as her parents' murderers wanted her dead, but she decided that maybe Jason could have been the target.

THE LOOSE SCREW
Gerald Hammond

After a motor smash, Beau Pepys and his cousin Jacqueline, her fiancé and dotty mother, suspect that someone had prearranged the death of their friend. But who, and why?

CASE WITH THREE HUSBANDS
Margaret Erskine

Was it a ghost of one of Rose Bonner's late husbands that gave her old Aunt Agatha such a terrible shock and then murdered her in her bed?

THE END OF THE RUNNING
Alan Evans

Lang continued to push the men and children on and on. Behind them were the men who were hunting them down, waiting for the first signs of exhaustion before they pounced.

CARNABY AND THE HIJACKERS
Peter N. Walker

When Commander Pigeon assigns Detective Sergeant Carnaby-King to prevent a raid on a bullion-carrying passenger train, he knows that there are traitors in high positions.

TREAD WARILY AT MIDNIGHT
Margaret Carr

If Joanna Morse hadn't been so hasty she wouldn't have been involved in the accident.

TOO BEAUTIFUL TO DIE
Martin Carroll

There was a grave in the churchyard to prove Elizabeth Weston was dead. Alive, she presented a problem. Dead, she could be forgotten. Then, in the eighth year of her death she came back. She was beautiful, but she had to die.

IN COLD PURSUIT
Ursula Curtiss

In Mexico, Mary and her cousin Jenny each encounter strange men, but neither of them realises that one of these men is obsessed with revenge and murder. But which one?

LITTLE DROPS OF BLOOD
Bill Knox

It might have been just another unfortunate road accident but a few little drops of blood pointed to murder.

GOSSIP TO THE GRAVE
Jonathan Burke

Jenny Clark invented Simon Sherborne because her daily gossip column was getting dull. Then Simon appeared at a party — in the flesh! And Jenny finds herself involved in murder.

HARRIET FAREWELL
Margaret Erskine

Wealthy Theodore Buckler had planned a magnificent Guy Fawkes Day celebration. He hadn't planned on murder.

SANCTUARY ISLE
Bill Knox

Chief Detective Inspector Colin Thane and Detective Inspector Phil Moss are sent to a bird sanctuary off the coast of Argyll to investigate the murder of the warden.

THE SNOW ON THE BEN
Ian Stuart

Although on holiday in the Highlands, Chief Inspector Hamish MacLeod begins an investigation when a pistol shot shatters the quiet of his solitary morning walk.

HARD CONTRACT
Basil Copper

Private detective Mike Farraday is hired to obtain settlement of a debt from Minsky. But Minsky is killed before Mike can get to him. A spate of murders follows.